W9-AYO-624

$22.95
F/FRO
Frost, Mark
Twin Peaks :
the final dossier

11/17

BRUMBACK LIBRARY
215 WEST MAIN STREET
VAN WERT, OHIO  45891

TWIN PEAKS: *The* FINAL DOSSIER

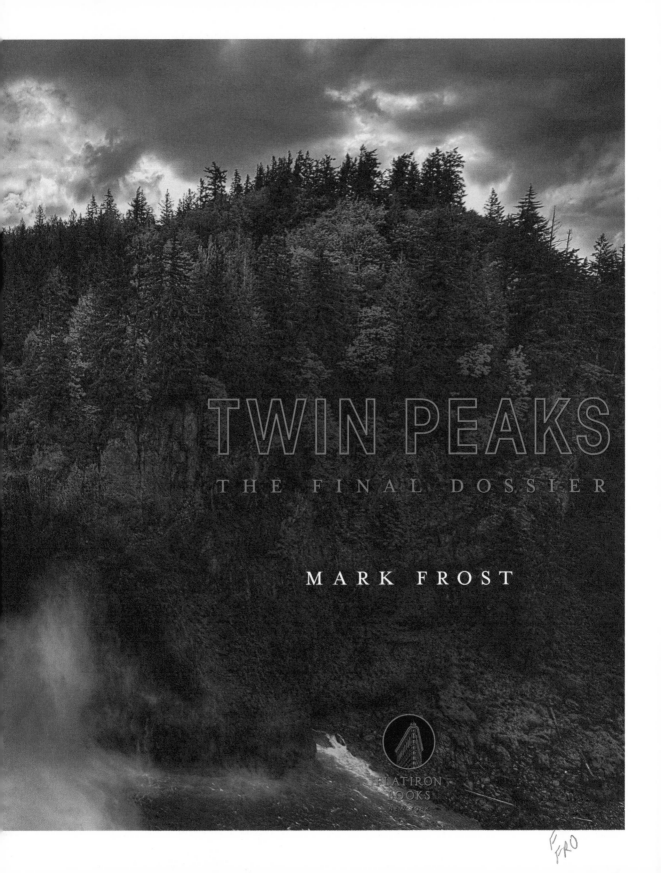

# TWIN PEAKS

## THE FINAL DOSSIER

### MARK FROST

FLATIRON
BOOKS
NEW YORK

This is a work of fiction. All of the characters, organizations,
and events portrayed in this novel are either products of the author's
imagination or are used fictitiously.

TWIN PEAKS: THE FINAL DOSSIER.

Copyright © 2017 by Mark Frost. All rights reserved.
Printed in the United States of America. For information, address
Flatiron Books, 175 Fifth Avenue, New York, N.Y. 10010.

www.flatironbooks.com

Front jacket and title page image by Kevin Franklin · Back jacket image "A Clearing
Winter Storm" © William Toti · Inside jacket image by Ken Crawford

All images from *Twin Peaks* courtesy of
Lynch/Frost Productions.

Designed by Paul Kepple, Max Vandenberg, and Marissa Raybuck at
HEADCASE DESIGN
www.headcasedesign.com

The Library of Congress Cataloging-in-Publication Data
is available upon request.

ISBN 978-1-250-16330-1 (hardcover)
ISBN 978-1-250-16331-8 (ebook)

Our books may be purchased in bulk for promotional,
educational, or business use. Please contact your local bookseller
or the Macmillan Corporate and Premium Sales Department
at 1-800-221-7945, extension 5442, or by email at
MacmillanSpecialMarkets@macmillan.com.

First Edition: October 2017

10 9 8 7 6 5 4 3 2 1

This is the seventeenth and last book I've created with the support, counsel, and unerring human intelligence of the late Ed Victor, my literary agent and good friend for thirty years. A lion of letters, literature, and culture, there's scarcely a publishing professional on two continents who has not benefited in some way from Ed's presence, influence, or companionship in their lives. Those of us fortunate enough to have been his clients will tell you those effects were never less than profound. For myself, I cannot imagine the journey I've followed—from aspiring writer to author—taking place without him.

There are, as always, many to thank for their help with this volume, but—just this once, in the wake of Ed's stunning absence—I defer those expressions of gratitude and ask Bob Miller, Colin Dickerman, Will Schwalbe, Paul Kepple, Marlena Bittner, and James Melia to join me in saluting a man who helped our business find its better self, and by doing so made this harsh world a kinder and more civilized place.

TWIN PEAKS: *The* FINAL DOSSIER

# INTEROFFICE MEMORANDUM

**DATE:**    September 6th, 2017

**FROM:**    TAMARA PRESTON, Special Agent

**TO:**    GORDON COLE, Deputy Director

Dear Director Cole:

Pursuant to your directive to me upon the completion of my investigation into "The Archivist's Dossier" last year, I hereby submit my subsequent follow-up report.

That archive—which ended abruptly on March 28, 1989, with the Major's sudden disappearance and presumed death—left us with many possible avenues of investigation. As you suggested to me at the time, I have since directed my own investigation "down every rabbit hole and up every apple tree" in search of answers. To state it more plainly, I'm "The Archivist" now.

Unlike the previous dossier, where for the most part all documents were presented to us in their entirety, per Bureau standards, here I have taken the time to condense the relevant content I found into an uninterrupted narrative.

As you also requested, I began this project in the town of Twin Peaks itself, by attempting to bring you up to date on the stories of many of the town's residents—many of whom you yourself knew personally—over the intervening decades. I learned much that was surprising— your words "these woods are full of secrets" come immediately to mind as a distinct understatement—and many other things reflecting the startling rate of change any community, small or large, faces over the course of a quarter century of recorded history.

The pace of change is extremely hard to perceive at close range—it's virtually invisible day-to-day—but viewed from a distance, it moves like lightning. The trials and trivialities of daily life, I've concluded, act on the mind as a kind of local anesthetic, numbing us to the relentless passage and ravages of time. I've also learned—a humbling admission, to be sure—to view this effect as a kind of mercy.

| DATE: | TOPIC: | | SUBMITTED BY: |
|-------|--------|--|---------------|
| 9/6/2017 | THE FINAL DOSSIER | | PRESTON, TAMARA |

SYNOPSIS OF FACTS:

My conclusions and takeaways from this part of the journey—which you also requested of me—I have included from time to time when they apply throughout the document, rather than offering them as a preamble, as I don't want to shade your perceptions prior to your first read.

On a personal level, I will share with you, however, that regardless of the cost to my innocence or naïveté regarding these truths of the human condition—which I now freely acknowledge at the start was "considerable"—I emerge from this experience grateful for the wisdom it has given me, and stronger of mind for the hard lessons learned.

May I also state that your faith in me to undertake this task, and the opportunity you've provided for me to contribute to the collective work that still lies ahead of us, remains one of the authentic blessings of my life.

I only hope that, in whatever small way I can, I'm able to apply my shoulder to that wheel for as long as time and fate allow.

Most respectfully yours,

*Tamara Preston*

Tamara Preston, Field Agent

Blue Rose Task Force

| APPROVED: | DO NOT WRITE IN THESE SPACES | | |
|-----------|------|------|------|
| CLASSIFIED | | | |

THE ADDENDUM:

This first document is, as you'll quickly learn, not exactly a "traditional" autopsy report. I assume this was made accessible to you at the time of the incident as a Blue Rose file, but since it was not passed along through traditional Bureau channels—and hardly embraces standard forensic formatting—I am including it in the pursuit of thoroughness.

## CALHOUN MEMORIAL HOSPITAL

# AUTOPSY REPORT

EXAMINATION REF. NO.

1989-04/01

JOHNSON, LEO ABEL

---

On the morning of April 1, 1989, an autopsy was completed on the body of LEO ABEL JOHNSON.

VISIBLE INJURIES: 5 gunshot wounds, numerous spider bites, electrical burns, bruises, cigarette burns

INTERNAL INJURIES: bullet lodged near spine, damage to sinus cavity

---

*Anatomical Summary:*

(A) 5 gunshot wounds to upper thoracic

(B) Arachnid bites; (Tarantula; Theraphosidae)

(C) Electrical burn marks

(D) Cigarette burns

(E) Bruising

(F) Bullet lodged internally near lower lumbar/3rd vertebra

CAUSE OF DEATH:
5 gunshot wounds (A)

*External Injuries Male (Front and Back):*

damage to sinus cavity

DATE AND SIGNATURE OF EXAMINER

*Albert Rosenfield*

SPECIAL AGENT ALBERT ROSENFIELD

76a3402-A12

It's not often I'm tempted to begin one of these by suggesting "he made the world a better place by taking early retirement," but in his case I'm willing to make an exception.

My own interaction with this knuckle-dragger was fleeting, but he left a vivid impression, not unlike the livid marks on his soon-to-be ex-wife's neck after he nearly strangled her. His entire life span could easily be written off as a scathing indictment of our public education system, but to be fair, you'd probably have to go all the way back to the crossroads where Cro-Magnon and Neanderthal went their separate ways and say: Leo's forbears took the path less traveled.

So, for starters: It wasn't the spiders that killed him. Whatever "evil genius"--I'm looking at you, Windom Earle--decided to hoist a bag of tarantulas over his head as a dire threat to Leo's health obviously wasted far too much time watching cheesy Vincent Price movies and not nearly enough studying arachnids. Tarantulas aren't ever fatally venomous, dipshit; they just look scary.

I'm going to go out on another limb and conclude that the five gunshots to his upper thoracic area had slightly more to do with the late, lamented Johnson's tragic demise. Patterned in a punctilious little circle around his heart, with one to grow on dead center. Unfortunately, aside from the killer, it appears that said spiders were the only witnesses.

Observations: The five nine-millimeter slugs were all still in the body--he had, I'll put it delicately, an excess of mass to help slam on the brakes--and there were no powder burns on his clothes or skin. Ergo, shot from across the room by someone with a low pulse and nifty marksmanship skills. Scuff marks near the door, where it appears the shooter set his feet Bureau style. Just a working theory--because who the hell knows where he's shuffled off to--but my money's all on our old pal Windom.

Also: Circular pattern of electrical burn marks around Leo's neck. A canine shock collar on the floor nearby, sized for a Saint Bernard. Nice: Leo must have made a first-rate slippers fetcher. Massive bruising over most of the body, cigarette burns, signs of malnutrition, even traces of birthday cake in his hair--I'm guessing these weren't all the residue of occupational hazard as a long-haul trucker. Windom enjoyed a lot of fun with the poor bastard.

initial _____

On the other hand, the damage to his nasal passages and sinus cavities--which look like a depleted uranium mine, 80 percent of the cartilage scorched or burned away-- appear to be entirely self-inflicted. Like the commercial almost says, things go better with crystal meth. That goes double if you're trying to keep your eyes peeled all night while hauling a load of cheap mattresses from Boise to Bishop.

This interested me: Leo also had a bullet lodged near the third vertebra of his lower lumbar spine. Conclusion: This is an earlier injury from a different weapon--from a .22 caliber--for which he had been treated some weeks earlier at the local hospital. The IC resident's diagnosis from that time noted Leo as suffering from paralysis of the extremities, but concluded that once surrounding inflammation subsided he might-- and apparently did--recover the use of his limbs, if not his senses.

So, you might well ask, who shot Leo the _first_ time?

According to the jacket meticulously assembled on our hero by--as they charitably refer to them here in East Rubesville--local law enforcement, Leo evolved from consumer to trafficker at some point in his sunset years. Going by the peek I took inside his cranium, impairment of moral judgment would have been the least of his symptomatic responses. He'd clearly suffered a cerebral hemorrhage within his last few weeks of life, but I'll spare you the clinical verbiage, Chief; his brain looks like a dog's breakfast, if your dog liked garbage with his scrambled eggs.

With his sudden departure, Leo Johnson left little behind aside from his badly used Corvette, bought a few months prior to death with a suspect amount of cash; the truck cab he used for his hauling business, repossessed by the leasing agency, postmortem; a ramshackle bungalow on the outskirts, also repo'd by the bank, postmortem; and his young widow, a hash slinger at the Double R Diner, Shelly McCauley Johnson. Known to you, I recall, as "the girl I'd most like to take to the prom."

By the way, forgive the stains on this page; writing this as I enjoy yet another delicious and oh-so-flaky chicken pot pie--third night in a row!--from that same local quarter-star bistro, the greasy spoon you keep raving about with the pie and the coffee. Pardon me, Gordon, but on the whole, to quote William Claude Dukenfield,

initial _____

I'd rather be in Philadelphia, where you are undoubtedly luxuriating at this very moment in your silk smoking jacket, enjoying a fruity French Bordeaux with another one of your imported "nieces."

Sorry. Trigger warning: Repeated and prolonged proximity to moribund logging communities set off my misanthropy. But indulge me long enough to offer a brief moment of sociological commentary: If the good folks of burgs like these would put down the remote and the beer or the bong and stay out of their "off-road vehicles" and duck blinds on weekends in order to punch the clock on some career counseling or community college, they might have a fighting chance to switch horses when the Turk comes to shutter their nineteenth-century industrial meal ticket. 'Cause the Turk is coming. The world is changing pronto, Chief, and now that these salt-of-the-earth "country volk" realize they've been left behind, it's going to be sheer hell playing catch-up. (I know, I know, I'm a raging asshole.)

And speaking of entrepreneurial initiative, here's a no-brainer: Why don't some of these enterprising yokels kick-start a craft brewery here in town? They'd instantly attract an endless stream of thirsty proles, and the only competition is swill.

Enough community building for one night. To sum up: Leo Johnson's dead. Having a hard time arguing that the local landscape isn't trending upward because of it.

Next case. Save me a glass, you cosmopolitan swell.

--Albert

PS: The recent body count from this little criminal corner of town is officially way off the actuarials: Jean Renault, Jacques Renault, Leo Johnson, and some other dirtbag drug dealer in the woods whose melodious name escapes me. When I brought this trend up to Sheriff Harry Truman--or, as I like to call him, Chatty Cathy--he replied: "Well...makes my job a whole lot easier."

initial _____ AR

# FEDERAL BUREAU OF INVESTIGATION

**CASE #**   008-072-0119        **BUREAU FILE #**   TP-01/18

# SHELLY JOHNSON

PRESTON, Tamara

**CASE AGENT**

INITIAL

# CONFIDENTIAL

FIELD OFFICE CRIMINAL INVESTIGATIVE
AND ADMINISTRATIVE FILES

See also Nos.  77-18-4500

FEDERAL BUREAU
OF INVESTIGATION

*Field Office Criminal Investigative
and Administrative Files*

SUBJECT

SHELLY JOHNSON

01

BUREAU FILE #
TP-01/18

DIVISION
PHL/PA

At a glance, Shelly's story reads as depressingly familiar: The only child of a dysfunctional local marriage that ended in early divorce, exacerbated by alcoholism and repeated incidents of spousal abuse. Shelly lived with her mother after the split—her father fled the state and disappeared—and Shelly left home for good at seventeen. While her Twin Peaks High School transcripts paint a portrait of a bright and promising student, she dropped out at the end of her junior year when Leo Johnson—six years her senior—suddenly careened into her life.

(My understanding is that you hold a personal fondness for Shelly, Chief, so I'm including a few more details here than I might have otherwise.)

According to a formal inquest conducted in the aftermath of Leo's death, these facts emerge:

A covert relationship between Shelly and Laura Palmer's putative boyfriend Bobby Briggs appears to have overlapped a large percentage of her nearly two-year marriage to Leo. Corroborated testimony also suggests that this relationship with Bobby during high school predated Leo: Bobby and Shelly were, in fact, contemporaries who had known each other going all the way back to elementary school.

One fellow student vividly recalled this: When Shelly realized Bobby was two-timing her with Laura, she confronted him in an angry public scene that disrupted the junior prom. She stormed out in her prom dress and, as fate would have it, decamped to a local adult venue known by its sign as the Bang Bang Bar, but more colloquially as The Roadhouse. Although she was underage at the time, a laissez-faire attitude toward the serving of underage patrons—it appears she knew the bartender on duty that night—resulted in Shelly downing a couple of beers before Leo Johnson, who had just rolled in from a road trip, intervened to gallantly procure for her a few more potent illicit cocktails, and before the night was over, one thing led to another.

CASE # 008-072-0119

TWIN PEAKS: THE FINAL DOSSIER

TOPIC

CLASSIFICATION
CONFIDENTIAL

FEDERAL BUREAU
OF INVESTIGATION

Cutting, as they say, to the chase, Leo and Shelly obtained the necessary paperwork and appeared before a local justice of the peace exactly three weeks later—the justice noted dryly in his remarks that the young couple stated they were "celebrating their third anniversary"—and tied the knot.

You might well ask: What could possibly go wrong? As we now know, everything that could did.

Within a few weeks of Leo's passing—let's charitably call this the observation of a designated mourning period—Shelly and Bobby began to appear together around town in public places, clearly a couple again, joined in grief, most assumed, by the deaths of their respective former partners.

I would, however, be remiss if I neglected to point out that, according to the case file, these two were also considered and subsequently cleared by law enforcement as prime suspects in Leo Johnson's murder. The emergence of at-large fugitive Windom Earle as the more probable culprit ultimately led investigators to conclude that, while evidence indicated they were far from blameless in Leo Johnson's downfall, Shelly and Bobby were, at best, not guilty and, at worst, seen as not likely to be successfully prosecuted.

One year after Leo's death, almost to the day—perhaps Shelly had learned something from the dictum "marry in haste, repent in leisure"—Bobby and Shelly were formally wed during a weekend getaway to Reno. Family did not attend.

Their now legal union, within seven months—timing that seems to have influenced this sudden decision to book a flight to Nevada—produced a daughter, Rebecca McCauley Briggs. Shelly's estranged mother died that same year, at forty-seven—cirrhosis of the liver—but Bobby's mother, Betty, grieving the recent loss of her own husband, stepped up to the plate, devoting herself to providing her son and his new wife a stability they sorely needed for their new family.

And as she had done since the day Shelly began working at the Double R, proprietor Norma Jennings—soon to lose her own hardened criminal husband, Hank, with far fewer regrets, in a prison shanking—played the role of the surrogate mother that Shelly had always needed. Norma and Betty joined forces to cosign a loan that allowed Bobby and Shelly to buy their first house. Within a year of Leo's death, when she turned twenty-one, Shelly now had a home, a husband she loved, a beautiful child, and a supportive circle of friends and customers at a job she adored. As the saying goes, it takes a diner to raise a child.

Of all the personal stories I've now surveyed in Twin Peaks, Shelly seems one of the luckiest ones. But then, as you well know, Chief, most stories have more than one act. I'll return to this one—and to Deputy Briggs—presently.

INITIAL *TP*   DATE 9, 6, 17

# FEDERAL BUREAU OF INVESTIGATION

CASE #  008-072-0119   BUREAU FILE #  TP-02/18

## HORNES AND
## HAYWARDS

PRESTON, Tamara

CASE AGENT

INITIAL

# CONFIDENTIAL

FIELD OFFICE CRIMINAL INVESTIGATIVE
AND ADMINISTRATIVE FILES

See also Nos.  53-77-987   8818
26387

FEDERAL BUREAU
OF INVESTIGATION

*Field Office Criminal Investigative
and Administrative Files*

During this same time frame, something curious and well under the radar occurred one night at the home of one of the town's most beloved citizens and its widely admired general practitioner, Dr. Will Hayward. I've assembled the following pieces of information I've been able to collate into the following scenario, which feels like the most reasonable explanation.

The event in question appears to have happened on the same day as the explosion in the vault of Twin Peaks Savings and Loan, which, as you'll remember from the dossier, resulted in the deaths of Pete Martell, Andrew Packard, and the bank's assistant manager, Dell Mibbler. That evening, the incident's only living survivor, Ben Horne's eighteen-year-old daughter, Audrey, gravely injured in the explosion, was being treated in intensive care at Calhoun Memorial Hospital. A closer examination yielded the following nine curiosities, reported below.

First curiosity: Also being treated for a serious head injury in the same ER that same night was Audrey's father, Ben Horne. Horne had spent most of the day in the hospital at Audrey's bedside but apparently left sometime after dark, only to return—as an urgent care patient—a little over an hour later.

Second curiosity: The admitting physician—who, it turns out, also drove Ben Horne to the hospital *after* his injury—was Dr. Will Hayward. The injury, according to Hayward's report, occurred at the Haywards' home, the result of a fall suffered when Horne—quoting the hospital admittance form—"slipped on the hearth of the living room fireplace, hitting his head on the hard granite mantel."

Hayward goes on to detail that Horne, despondent over his daughter's condition, had come to the house "seeking counsel" about his daughter's chances for recovery. (Why this conversation never took place at the hospital, where both men spent most of the day together, is neither asked nor answered.)

BUREAU FILE #

TP-02 / 18

DIVISION

PHL / PA

After rapidly consuming a couple of drinks, served by the doctor himself, Horne complained of feeling "light-headed" and, moments later, collapsed in front of the Hayward fireplace. The doctor goes on to mention that he and Horne had been speaking privately at the time, so there were no other witnesses.

Third curiosity: The only medical file I've been able to obtain from the hospital is brief, almost cursory, and was also written by Dr. Hayward. There is a reference to X-rays being taken, presumably to check for skull fractures—results negative—but I have been unable to find them. There is no mention of any other specific symptoms to support Dr. Hayward's diagnosis that Ben Horne had suffered a "grade 2 concussion" and his recommendation that he be held in the hospital overnight for observation. Horne was admitted to a room just down the hallway from the one occupied by his injured daughter. With everything else going on in town that day—the bank explosion, Agent Cooper's overnight disappearance and return—local law enforcement was stretched fairly thin, so it appears that no officials ever questioned the doctor's account of Ben Horne's injury.

Fourth curiosity: We now know that the next morning, Doc Hayward accompanied Sheriff Truman to examine Agent Cooper in his room at the Great Northern Hotel, after he returned from a mysterious night spent—exact whereabouts unknown—in the Ghostwood National Forest. While they were in the room—again according to Doc Hayward's subsequent report—Agent Cooper went to the bathroom to brush his teeth, slipped on the bathroom floor, and slammed his head into the mirror over the sink, knocking himself unconscious. Once again, Doc Hayward accompanied his patient to the hospital—this time Sheriff Truman drove—and admitted him with the same diagnosis: a grade 2 concussion. While they were there, according to the hospital log timeline, Ben Horne was discharged—after being examined and cleared for release by the on-call doctor; *not* Doc Hayward—and was taken home by his brother, Jerry.

Fifth curiosity: Agent Cooper, according to available records, spent that day and night in the hospital before checking himself out—without receiving medical clearance—the following morning. Within two days, he would vanish from Twin Peaks and disappear from view for the next quarter of a century. We also know—from a report filed by Sheriff Frank Truman more than twenty-five years later—that at some point that day, while making his rounds, Doc

Hayward saw Cooper in a hospital corridor, fully dressed in his usual black suit, exiting the room in the ICU occupied by Audrey Horne.

Sixth curiosity: Nine months later, almost to the day, Audrey Horne gave birth to her son Richard Horne. The birth certificate states the identity of the father as "unknown."

Seventh curiosity: Within two days, Agent Cooper had vanished, and Major Garland Briggs—reportedly the last person in town whom Cooper visited before his disappearance—had been declared dead after a fire at Listening Post Alpha, high up in the mountains of the Ghostwood Forest. Although the charred corpse found at the scene was too damaged to identify through then relatively nascent DNA technology, the discovery of a few loose teeth, which matched Briggs's dental records, led to the conclusion that he had indeed died in the fire, the cause of which, the subsequent intensive Bureau investigation concluded, remains "unknown."

Eighth curiosity: Within three months of these apparently interrelated events, the following events occurred. After a lifetime spent in the state of Washington, without warning, Doc Hayward abruptly shuttered his thriving practice and moved all the way across the country to the town of Middlebury, Vermont. Shortly thereafter, Hayward and his wife, Eileen, after twenty-six years of marriage, filed papers that finalized an uncontested and mutually agreed-upon divorce. In that same month, their oldest daughter, Donna— just after graduating with honors from Twin Peaks High—also left town for good, settling in New York City. Her mother, still confined to a wheelchair after a car accident nearly two decades earlier, remained in the Hayward family's Twin Peaks home, where she raised their two younger daughters, Harriet and Gersten, alone.

Ninth curiosity: I have identified a steady flow of income—$7,500 a month—into the bank account of Eileen Hayward. The payments began the month that Doc Hayward left town and persisted until Eileen's death, from pneumonia, in 2009. These appear to have been direct-deposit wire transfers from an offshore account in the Cayman Islands. I have just traced that account to a shell LLC corporation registered to the Horne Foundation.

As of this writing, the foundation's principal, Benjamin Horne—responding through his attorney—has denied my repeated requests for an interview on this subject. Since the filings were all made in accordance with existing law, and there is no apparent appearance of a crime or corporate malfeasance, DOJ has declined to issue a subpoena to pursue this matter.

My feeling—not entirely supported by fact—is that something untoward happened in the Hayward household that night when Benjamin Horne dropped in. The effects of this event seem to have devastated—and effectively destroyed—one of the community's most admired and respected families. Harriet seems to have suffered the fewest ill effects; after high school, she studied at the University of Washington, eventually becoming a pediatrician in the Bellevue area, a suburb of Seattle. Gersten I'll return to in a moment.

INITIAL *TP*    DATE 9, 6, 17

# FEDERAL BUREAU OF INVESTIGATION

CASE # **008-072-0119**    BUREAU FILE # **TP-03/18**

# DONNA HAYWARD

PRESTON, Tamara

**CASE AGENT**

*TP*

INITIAL

# CONFIDENTIAL

FIELD OFFICE CRIMINAL INVESTIGATIVE
AND ADMINISTRATIVE FILES

See also Nos. 53 –77–987
0392
44–26

FEDERAL BUREAU
OF INVESTIGATION

Arriving in New York City in 1992, Donna Hayward began taking undergraduate classes at Hunter College. She had just turned eighteen. She supported herself by working as a model, eventually signing with the exclusive Ford modeling agency. All reports indicate that during this time she cut off all communication with both her father and her mother, exchanging letters and occasional phone calls only with her younger sisters. She similarly cut off contact with all of her former friends in Twin Peaks, with one exception: A few years later, she exchanged two letters with Audrey Horne. (I learned this from Donna herself, replying by written letter, not email, to my repeated inquiries to her. She was unwilling to share the letters with me, or discuss any of their content.)

As her modeling career advanced, Donna dropped out of Hunter College after her freshman year. The job carried her to various foreign countries, and she worked in Paris, Milan, Monaco, and other fashion meccas. Within the industry she was considered one of the "fresh faces" of the nineties—after the somewhat decadent previous decade—a return to a more wholesome all-American look, perhaps best epitomized by Kathy Ireland.

To be blunt, Donna had taken a hard left into the fast lane. During this time, she frequently appeared in the gossip and society columns of various New York newspapers, where she was linked romantically with a variety of high-profile men: a soap opera star, a professional tennis player, a night-club magnate, and a minor and somewhat dissolute scion of a European royal family.

Near the end of the decade, as she reached her late twenties and her modeling career slowed, Donna married a man nearly two decades her senior, the cofounder of a successful dot-com startup and a prominent figure in the New York venture capital community. If anything, this raised her social profile ever further, as the couple entertained frequently at their Sutton Place brownstone and their opulent beach house in Southampton.

Just before the turn of the century, at an unspecified charity event on one of these weekends, Donna apparently encountered Lana Budding Milford, the widow of *Twin Peaks Post* publisher Douglas Milford. Both wearing couture and wide smiles, their photo ran on the society page of the *New York Post*. While Lana appears to beam, on closer examination, something around the edges of Donna's expression appears fraught with tension and dismay.

Whether this encounter had any direct bearing on what happened next is impossible to determine, but Donna's fairy-tale New York existence—polo, yachts, helicopters, the whole nine yards of garish material excess—unraveled shortly thereafter, exposing the reality of a much harsher inner life: Four years into the marriage, Donna discreetly and, at first, voluntarily entered rehab for drug and alcohol dependence.

This proved to be only the first of Donna's four stints in rehab over the next five years—the last of which, an involuntary stay at McLean psychiatric hospital, in Massachusetts, was the result of an intervention. This final episode—in which she was reported missing by her husband, then found two days later in a Lower East Side crack house—appears to have been triggered by the death from heart failure of her mother, Eileen, with whom Donna had never reconciled nor, as near as I can determine, spoken in the seventeen years since her sudden departure from Twin Peaks. Donna did not attend the funeral.

Shortly after her release from McLean, sober now but shaky, Donna's husband initiated divorce proceedings. Because she had signed an ironclad prenuptial agreement, Donna was awarded only a low-six-figure lump sum and a modest monthly stipend. She soon moved into an apartment in a suburb of New Haven, Connecticut, far from the limelight in which she'd been living, where she rigorously attended local 12-step meetings and managed to hang on to her sobriety.

Approaching forty and facing an uncertain future, Donna at this point reached out to her father, Will Hayward, for the first time in more than twenty years. This contact, it seems, led to their reconciliation. Within a year, Donna had moved to the small college town of Middlebury, Vermont, where Will—now well into his seventies—was still practicing family medicine. Donna moved in with her father and began working as his assistant in his practice. Doc Hayward, in the past year, has quietly begun to wind down his daily hours but says he intends to never fully retire. Donna remains by his side to this day, living a quiet life and very active as a sponsor in the local 12-step community. Although she politely rebuffed all of my attempts to speak to her directly, I've learned she is currently studying to obtain a degree as a nurse practitioner.

I should mention that Donna's youngest sister, Gersten, has, if anything, suffered even more obvious ill effects from whatever events tore this family apart. Gersten was an exceptional child in many regards; a musical prodigy, she performed as a piano soloist in concert venues all across the Northwest while still in her early teens. She was also a prodigiously talented mathematician, taking college-level courses while still a high school freshman; she graduated from high school at sixteen and was offered scholarships from a number of prominent universities. Able to speak and read four languages fluently, Gersten has been tested well above genius level in IQ.

Throughout her childhood and teen years, her exceptionalism in so many disciplines appeared to function as a kind of shield from the turbulence and unhappiness that descended on her family. Once she entered Stanford University, at sixteen, however, it quickly became apparent that the energy put into all of these high-stress/high-function abilities did not protect her from whatever trauma she'd suffered as a child, nor did it prepare her emotionally for the internal demands this more adult world was now placing on her. By the middle of her second semester, after exhibiting alarming symptoms of maladaptation to her new circumstances, Gersten suffered what was diagnosed as a severe nervous collapse and emotional breakdown.

After six weeks of treatment in a Bay Area psychiatric hospital, she was released, withdrew from Stanford, and returned home to Twin Peaks to live with her mother. Gersten underwent immediate and ongoing psychiatric care, and her health improved, but sadly, her ability to cope with the trials of everyday living did not. Although doctors had prescribed for her a steady course of antidepressants as an ongoing protocol, during this period Gersten privately turned to stronger street drugs for comfort, concurrent with the nationwide trend in dependence on opioids and designer synthetics. The death of her mother, Eileen, in 2009, by removing her protective influence and the social safety net Gersten had come to depend upon, appeared to derange her even further. This led her into a series of reckless and chaotic relationships with a number of men and women. The most damaging of these proved to be an off-again, on-again affair with one Steven Burnett, an unstable career miscreant and low-level drug dealer in the Twin Peaks area, who had in the interim become her primary source for narcotics.

This relationship preceded and apparently also overlapped Steven's marriage to Rebecca Briggs, daughter of Shelly and Bobby Briggs. Now in her early twenties, Becky works at a bakery owned by Norma Jennings in downtown Twin Peaks. A warrant for Steven Burnett was recently issued as a suspected accomplice in an international drug-running operation—he has gone missing—that prominently involved Audrey's son, Richard Horne—who is also still at large and wanted on, among other things, a hit-and-run warrant—and a crooked deputy in the Twin Peaks Sheriff's Department, Chad Broxford, who is currently awaiting trial on a variety of charges. The timely intervention of her mother, Shelly, and her father, Deputy Sheriff Bobby Briggs, appears to have spared Becky any lasting legal trouble, but Gersten has not been seen since and is believed to have left the area.

INITIAL TP DATE 9 / 6 / 17

# FEDERAL BUREAU OF INVESTIGATION

04

18

CASE #  008-072-0119     BUREAU FILE #      TP-04/18

# BEN AND AUDREY
# HORNE

PRESTON, Tamara

**CASE AGENT**

INITIAL *TP*

# CONFIDENTIAL

FIELD OFFICE CRIMINAL INVESTIGATIVE
AND ADMINISTRATIVE FILES

See also Nos.  53-77-987
44-26
3311

FEDERAL BUREAU
OF INVESTIGATION

*Field Office Criminal Investigative
and Administrative Files*

Nothing would please my longing for narrative closure more than to report that Audrey Horne's near-death experience at the bank resulted in a meaningful reconciliation with her father, Ben. Sadly, this does not appear to be the case. The unknown seismic shifts that led to the dissolution of the Hayward marriage appeared to cause a kind of bank-shot collateral damage to the Hornes' thirty-year union as well. Having already lived separate lives, by most accounts, for more than a decade, Ben and Sylvia Horne divorced within two years of the Haywards' dissolution. Both remained in the Twin Peaks area: Ben kept the old family house, and Sylvia moved across town to a McMansion in a gated, upscale housing development where she has ever since assumed sole custody and care of their special-needs son, Johnny—a profound case of autism—who is now in his early forties.

Audrey awoke from the coma she'd been in as a result of the bank explosion after three and a half weeks. She apparently retained no memory of the event itself, and at first seemed to be on her way to a complete recovery. Two events altered that trajectory. First was her father's decision to proceed with the sale of the Horne family's privately owned 350-acre parcel of the Ghostwood Forest—the sale Audrey had been protesting against when she went into the bank that morning—to a secretive investment capital group that immediately began construction of a privately owned and operated state prison on the site. Then Audrey discovered, two months after her release from the hospital, that she was pregnant.

Audrey refused all offers of financial help from her father and mother, moved out of the family home and into a small apartment, and prepared, as she put it in a letter to her mother at the time, for the most important role of her life: raising her child as a single mother. Audrey had just turned nineteen when her son, Richard, was born. She never returned to high school, completing her GED through independent study over the next two years. She then enrolled in classes at the local community college, studying economics and business administration.

After obtaining her degree, she opened a local hair and beauty salon in the Twin Peaks area, which she has successfully owned and operated ever since. She had few friends, outside of her customers and employees, and largely kept to herself. She never commented publicly—and was never heard to speculate with anyone—about who the father of her son might be, and didn't seem interested in discussing it with anyone. If Audrey herself was curious about the father's identity, she never availed herself of any easily obtained paternity test that I've been able to uncover. One could conclude that she didn't care, or perhaps she knew who it was all along. (The only possible clue I've been able to find along these lines is a framed photo of Agent Cooper that hangs on the wall of her office at the salon.)

True to her word, although her mother, Sylvia, played an important role as Richard's grandmother, Audrey raised the boy entirely on her own. She has apparently never allowed her son to meet his grandfather Ben. Circumstances changed after Richard's tenth birthday, when, without warning, in a private civil ceremony, Audrey married her longtime accountant. Witnesses close to the situation suggest that this was more a marriage of financial convenience than affection, and during my research here I've come across troubling accounts of public scenes, heavy drinking, verbal abuse, and sexual infidelity—all allegedly on the wife's part. The couple briefly consulted a marriage counselor, and Audrey apparently consulted her own mental health care professional during this time, but those files are sealed and inaccessible. Four years ago, without warning, Audrey closed the salon. Not long after she seemed to vanish from public life, into either agorophobic seclusion, or—one troubling rumor suggests—a private care facility. The Horne family spokesperson has refused to respond to all inquiries regarding her whereabouts.

Ben Horne spends the majority of his time at the Great Northern Hotel, where he keeps a private suite for his personal use but just as often sleeps in his office. He appears to spend as little time in the old nearby family manse as possible; his brother, Jerry, still resides in his own private wing there. Ben remains as active in his various businesses as ever, but since the sale of their portion of the Ghostwood Forest—and the impact it had on his daughter's life—it seems clear that he has conducted his investments and purchases on a more readily apparent ethical footing.

He also remains deeply troubled by the project that was eventually put up on the former Horne land in Ghostwood. The privately held and run prison opened there in 2001, a deeply controversial project not just in the town but regionwide. Owned through a shell company by an opaque consortium of conservative investors in the Midwest, this company has proved itself an absentee landlord in the worst sense of the word. An ugly, brutish structure— built by lowball contractors to save money—the Ghostwood Correctional Facility is widely considered the ugliest object in this otherwise pristine valley. Ben Horne himself has, on more than one occasion, publicly referred to it as "a blight on our land." While the prison has provided some low-wage, low-skill employment opportunities for many area workers displaced by the shuttering of the local logging industry, it is by all accounts dispiriting work for a company with little apparent regard for employee relations. When workers attempted to unionize in the early part of this century, the company simply refused to recognize their right to bargain collectively, and threatened to bus in workers from out of state. The strategy proved effective, and the employees backed down. The arrival of the prison coincided with a sharp rise within the local community in a number of medical issues: alcoholism, depression, prescription opioid addiction and abuse, illegal trafficking in same, domestic violence, and suicide. A majority of those affected by these issues are prison employees and their families. A *Twin Peaks Post* editorial has referred to this ongoing tragedy as an epidemic.

(Interesting footnote: The chief administrator of Ghostwood prison at this time, Warden Dwight Murphy, crossed our radar during the recent Blue Rose investigation. It may be worth our time to see if his subsequent murder related back in any way to his years at Ghostwood.)

My personal interview with Ben Horne at the Great Northern—which, surprisingly, he agreed to—revealed a man on the cusp of old age, rueful and filled with regrets for what he sees as his many failings. He openly claims to take full responsibility for the damage wrought upon his family and remains unwilling to blame anything or anyone but himself. He also seems moved by an urgent impulse to find a more spiritual direction for his life, and mentioned that he's trying to spend more time out in nature than he's been accustomed to. My impression, in this regard, is that he feels the weight of narrowing time pressing down and seems eager to make amends.

For all this, Ben Horne's chief regret—or, at least, one that he was willing to express to me personally—remains the sale of the family's section of the Ghostwood Forest. Having paid a visit there recently, I can personally attest that Ghostwood Correctional Facility is more than just a befouling presence in the once pristine foothills of Blue Pine Mountain. Its long record of ignoring employee complaints places it in the lowest 10 percent among the burgeoning phenomenon of private prisons nationwide. Widespread reports of abuse and neglect toward its inmates place it even closer to rock bottom. I am also looking into rumors of alleged collusion between the prison's parent company and some regional police forces—*not* including, I hasten to add, the Twin Peaks Sheriff's Department—to step up arrest rates and stiffen conviction recommendations on relatively minor offenses, in order to increase what is referred to in company literature as "the prison's client population." As an aside, this is a potentially explosive issue that should concern any dedicated law enforcement personnel, one that I believe warrants our attention nationwide.

INITIAL *TP*  DATE 9/6/17

# FEDERAL BUREAU OF INVESTIGATION

CASE #   008-072-0119          BUREAU FILE #   TP-05/18

# JERRY HORNE

PRESTON, Tamara

**CASE AGENT**

INITIAL

# CONFIDENTIAL

FIELD OFFICE CRIMINAL INVESTIGATIVE
AND ADMINISTRATIVE FILES

See also Nos. 312-20-53
6293          26387

FEDERAL BUREAU
OF INVESTIGATION

*Field Office Criminal Investigative
and Administrative Files*

Ben's younger brother, Jerry Horne, his longtime junior partner in business—if not in crime; although Ben has faced accusations of malfeasance many times in the past, let it be stated for the record that neither man has ever come under any felony indictment—has chosen a distinctly different path in the past two decades. A lifelong bachelor, Jerry seems to have floated through his privileged existence without forming any lasting romantic attachments; a string of shorter, more ephemeral affairs of the heart he has amassed in abundance. He remains to this day an enthusiastic world traveler—he is conversationally adept in four languages—and appears to have perpetually filled the role of "advance man" for the family business, bringing in deals from companies throughout the States and, indeed, the globe (Denmark, Finland, Brazil, Norway, France, and Morocco, to name just a few). In other words, Jerry roped 'em in—often lavishly hosting and entertaining clients at the Great Northern Hotel, often referred to in company PR as "the crown jewel of the family's portfolio"—where Ben assumed the more senior position of the "closer." A word-cloud analysis of news stories written about Ben's colorful younger brother over the years yields the following: *gadfly, cheerful, enthusiastic, restless, upbeat, good-natured, wild man, spontaneous, life of the party*. You get the idea. Whether any of the Hornes' many and varied business ventures ever actually originated with Jerry alone is hard to determine.

With one notable exception. Over the past ten years, Jerry has originated and pursued one new business venture that is, without a doubt, entirely the result of his own initiative. This operation also appears poised, as a result of rapidly changing social and legal conventions, to become on paper the most massively successful endeavor in Horne Corp. history. One may decide to credit "bohemian" Jerry with no more than wishful thinking, but he did accurately anticipate the legalization of marijuana dawning in the state of Washington. More than that, he was, in fact, one of that movement's major donors and behind-the-scene organizers for many years before the official legislation finally passed in 2012. Anecdotally, it appears that motivation for his activism went well beyond the libertarian or fiduciary into the personal; by which I mean Jerry, according to a number of sources I've heard from, has been perpetually as high as an orbiting communications satellite since approximately 1969.

(For instance, just a small sample of the available confirming evidence: As a college student—Gonzaga, class of '68—Jerry drove cross-country to attend Woodstock in his own private customized Airstream trailer. He appears briefly in the Oscar-winning documentary of that landmark concert, literally emerging from the Airstream with a bevy of nubile hippie chicks in a cloud of smoke. He was for years a known associate of renowned Oregon-based author Ken Kesey—*One Flew Over the Cuckoo's Nest*—a notorious libertine and sixties-style consciousness-raising advocate, as a member of his ragtag entourage of followers, known collectively as the Merry Pranksters. A title which, come to think of it, is as concise a distillation of Jerry Horne's essence as I could hope to express. For example: Jerry once attempted to obtain a medical license for marijuana use—years before it became legal for that purpose—in order to treat his "addiction to marijuana.")

Because he acted with uncharacteristic discipline and focus, Jerry's preparation meshed perfectly with opportunity, resulting in Washington State's most successful domestic cannabis production outfit in a—pardon the phrase, Chief—highly competitive and tightly regulated business environment. Jerry had privately dabbled for decades as an amateur botanist—"growing your own," as they say in the "medicinal" community—and, since legalization, has personally developed more than a dozen distinct Frankenstein strains and hybrids of alarming potency. (Among his most popular, to illustrate the point: "Whose Hands Are These?"; "Collateral Damage"; and "The Center Will Not Hold.") The net effect of this has made his products among the most sought-after in the marketplace, and a recent announcement that he has plans to open a string of brick-and-mortar retail shops (name TBD, but among the domain names he has already reserved: "AHigherCalling.com," "EightMilesHigh.com," and "UpUpandAway.com") indicates he's positioning the operation for a move into the regional and, they hope, national market as cannabis laws grow progressively less prohibitive.

Jerry has undoubtedly mellowed with time and age, an effect that shouldn't surprise, given that by this point he must have stockpiled levels of THC in his system that could preserve a woolly mammoth. He remains, as he's always been, a loner by nature, given to long stretches wandering in the nearby wilderness—his only friend outside of the Horne family appears to be Dr. Lawrence Jacoby (more on this relationship to come). At this time, he has no "significant other" in his life. The most recent in his long string of paramours, Jasmin Caspari, a self-styled "Jungian tantric Rolfer" from Switzerland, returned home to Lake Geneva a few months ago. Jerry's hobbies include butterfly collecting, bird-watching, and baking—which one suspects may have a correlating professional component—and he's also a fanatical audiophile. His collection of original and reissued vinyl literally fills a barn, one of a collection of deluxe private cabins he owns next to a small lake far up in the woods above Twin Peaks, where, legend has it, he once collaborated with famed Canadian rocker Neil Young to build a custom sound system that effectively turned two of these cabins into gigantic speakers, utilizing a woodshed as a subwoofer.

Jerry has been known to paddle a canoe out into the middle of the lake, activate the system by remote control, and crank up the volume—as the saying goes—to eleven. The resulting wall of sound from certain recordings is rumored to create whitecaps on the water and terrify most of the indigenous wildlife within a five-mile radius. (Dr. Jacoby was once heard to mention, on his pirate radio show, that one winter Jerry's blasting of Miles Davis's album *Bitches Brew* at top volume triggered a small avalanche.)

| INITIAL | DATE |
|---|---|
| *TP* | 9, 6, 17 |

# FEDERAL BUREAU OF INVESTIGATION

CASE # **008-072-0119**          BUREAU FILE # **TP-06/18**

# THE DOUBLE R

PRESTON, Tamara

**CASE AGENT**

*TP*

INITIAL

# CONFIDENTIAL

FIELD OFFICE CRIMINAL INVESTIGATIVE
AND ADMINISTRATIVE FILES

See also Nos. 001-43-25
2663
4828

FEDERAL BUREAU
OF INVESTIGATION

*Field Office Criminal Investigative
and Administrative Files*

I've identified a curious piece of either misdirection or misinformation in Major Briggs's dossier—or rather the section of the dossier that Briggs attributes to Agent Cooper, two stand-alone chapters about the Andrew Packard case that Briggs claimed to have found in a composition notebook stored in the Book-house library. The reason for the discrepancy I've uncovered—whether indicative of either man being misled by his sources on this, or the result of his own personal sense of discretion smoothing over a deeply sensitive personal matter—is difficult to pinpoint. (There may also be a motive for this related to a high-level security issue; I'll elaborate later.) I have my own theory about the reason but will let you be the judge.

On page ten of Cooper's story, he mentions that Norma Jennings's father, Marty—owner and founder of the Double R Diner—had been "diagnosed with heart disease" and that Norma's mother, Ilsa, "left the diner to care for him," effectively leaving Norma to run the diner on her own. Three paragraphs later, on the following page, without specifying the circumstances, Cooper writes: "Norma lost her dad in 1978." From what we've learned on the previous page, one would naturally conclude from this that Marty Lindstrom had passed away.

One thorny problem: Upon further review, I've been unable to confirm this news from any other primary, secondary, or tertiary source. No obituary for Marty Lindstrom appears in the *Twin Peaks Post* or any other newspaper in the region in 1978. There are no records or mentions of services rendered or conducted at any mortuaries in the area, nor could I find a contemporary death certificate here or in any neighboring county that corresponds to either this time frame or this set of circumstances. Further, no gravestone for Marty Lindstrom can be found in any of Twin Peaks' three largest cemeteries.

In the next paragraph, Cooper's story goes on to say, "Ilsa never got over losing Marty," that her health subsequently failed, and that she died in her sleep in 1984. This much, anyway, I have been able to verify: Ilsa Lindstrom passed when he said she did, at which point Norma inherited the diner.

What I have since uncovered is a trail of evidence leading to a wholly different narrative outcome—one that confirms the idea of "heart trouble" at the core of the family's breakdown, but of an entirely different variety. Chief, a word of warning: This is not a happy story, it doesn't begin or end well, and the middle is equally dreadful.

As mentioned in numerous histories of the Double R, prior to founding his restaurant, Marty Lindstrom for twenty-five years worked for the Union Pacific Railroad. It appears he never quite got the wanderlust inspired by a career spent riding the rails out of his blood (emphasis on *lust*). Since at least the early 1970s, Marty had been taking extended two-to-three-day trips away from Twin Peaks by train—as a retirement perk, he had been given a lifetime rail pass—at least twice a month, along with at least two weeklong solitary "vacations" annually. These trips were made, almost without exception, to the Yakima area, a couple of hundred miles to the southwest, where Marty was said to maintain other business interests, including a vintage roadside motel he allegedly purchased out of bankruptcy in the late 1960s.

I have confirmed that Marty Lindstrom did indeed own the deed and title of a motel on Highway 24, east of Yakima, called the Weary Traveler. Marty's more compelling interest in the property, however, appears to have been an ambitious thirty-something woman by the name of Vivian Smith, who at the time managed said motel for him. At some point at least five years prior to 1978, Marty's wife, Ilsa, appears to have discovered the truth about her husband's double life, which coincides neatly with the onset of his so-called heart disease. It proved to be a fatal case, at least to the Lindstroms' marriage; Marty left his business and family and Twin Peaks for good in 1978—the same year, as Cooper wrote, that Norma "lost" him. At which point Marty set up permanent housekeeping with Vivian Smith at the Weary Traveler, and, since Ilsa refused to grant him a divorce, their shacking up continued to be of the common-law variety.

Ilsa's principled denial apparently enraged the socially climbing Vivian—the only daughter of two high school teachers, herself a failed and thwarted former actress and singer from the Seattle area—who took that anger out on Marty, regularly and viciously, according to accounts I've sourced from two former Weary Traveler employee witnesses. A remorseful, guilt-ridden Marty—apparently all too aware he'd made a royal hash of his and his family's life—withered under Vivian's relentless assault and did indeed leave this life in 1985, less than a year after learning that his abandoned wife had passed away in Twin Peaks.

Marty assigned Vivian all ownership and rights to the Weary Traveler in his last legal will. He also left her with the twelve-year-old daughter Vivian had given birth to in 1973 as a result of their illicit coupling. Her name was Annie, and her arrival lines up perfectly with the onset of Marty's regular trips to Yakima. Annie's birth certificate bears her mother's last name, Smith, and she grew up in and around the motel, apparently without ever being informed that Marty was her actual father. Witnesses told me that Vivian told Annie throughout her early years that Marty Lindstrom was her uncle.

Norma didn't know about any of this, either, until, it seems, her mother, Ilsa, made at least a partial deathbed confession to her in 1984. At which point Norma decided to reach out to Marty, with whom she'd barely spoken—and she had seen him only once—in the six years since he'd split Twin Peaks and the Double R. It was not a happy reunion, as she apparently found her father at the Weary Traveler in severely reduced physical and mental health. She also discovered that, with Ilsa now dead and gone, Vivian had finally, and hastily, persuaded the obviously dying and mentally diminished Marty to marry her. (Vivian had, in the meantime, marginally upscaled her all-too-common maiden name to its cousin, the more aspirational Smythe.)

During her visit, Norma was also stunned to learn that she had a twelve-year-old half sister who had grown up in painfully tough and tawdry circumstances, with a full complement of psychic scars and emotional fragility to show for it. The shock of this discovery marshaled the essential goodness of Norma's character into a strong protective instinct toward the girl. Annie responded immediately to some of the only offered kindness she'd ever known, and a permanent loving bond formed between them. For many years, Norma declined to share this secret with either her husband, Hank, or the secret love of her own life, Big Ed Hurley. But for the good of the girl, Norma kept this connection with Annie alive, and in order to help herself cope, she went to extraordinary efforts to maintain a civil relationship with Vivian, the woman who had played such a callous, unfeeling role in the destruction of her own family.

Less than six weeks after Marty's death, Vivian Smythe Lindstrom married the owner of a successful beer distribution company from the Yakima area

named Roland Blackburn, a handsome, chiseled country club lout with a drinking problem and a violent temper. (There's more than ample reason to suspect that Roland had openly entered into a relationship with her while Marty was still living.) Vivian moved out of the motel and into Blackburn's manicured suburban estate with her daughter. A few weeks after they set up house, Blackburn officially adopted Annie, and a few days after that, they shipped her off to an almost medievally cloistered Catholic boarding school in Kennewick, Washington, about a hundred miles to the east. According to school records, the only relative who ever visited Annie during her first year at the school was Norma. During the time she spent there, away from her mother and stepfather, Annie seemed to stabilize; her grades were close to the top of her class, and school records invariably describe her as a bright and eager student.

Three years later, in her senior year, during a visit home for Christmas, something happened after a holiday party one night between Annie and her stepfather. Details are hazy on this, but my reading is this: most likely an attempted sexual assault after a night of heavy drinking. Piecing the story together from police reports and various witness accounts, this assault seems to have either been discovered or interrupted by Vivian, resulting in what one can imagine must have been a devastating confrontation.

His response: Roland Blackburn stormed out of their house, jumped into his deluxe Cadillac DeVille, and within fifteen minutes drove it off a bridge into the frigid Yakima River. The car was retrieved, and Blackburn was declared dead at the scene. Insurance investigators took a long, hard look at the incident; it might have been a suicide, which would have voided Blackburn's hefty insurance policy. Vivian offered a convincing denial to both the police and the insurance company that anything was troubling Blackburn to that extreme. There was also some evidence—impossible to confirm because of severe damage from the accident—that the car's brake line may have been tampered with, suggesting foul play, but the report concluded there was not enough evidence to provoke criminal charges. The insurance company was forced to make good on the policy.

But the damage was far from over: Annie Blackburn attempted suicide the night after Roland's death by downing a bottleful of tranquilizers and slitting her wrists with a box cutter. Discovered by her mother, she was rushed to a local hospital, where they pumped her stomach, stanched the bleeding, and saved her life. Annie remained unresponsive—and borderline catatonic—after the incident, and doctors soon diagnosed her as having suffered a disabling nervous breakdown. Acting on doctors' recommendations, Vivian arranged for Annie to be treated and confined in a psychiatric hospital in western Washington—coincidentally, the same one where Nadine Hurley and her mother had both been treated years earlier.

Annie spent six months in this facility, undergoing regular psychiatric care and psychological counseling. After Vivian signed her in and dropped her off, once again the only family member who visited Annie regularly was her half sister, Norma. During those months, Vivian became romantically entangled with a charming and shady drifter named Ernie Niles, who one day showed up at the doorstep of the Weary Traveler. A breezy, amiable con man—with a long rap sheet—Ernie quickly zeroed in on Vivian's apparent vulnerability. Sizing her up as a bereaved widow overwhelmed by circumstance and struggling to run her own business, he sold himself as just the guy to help her out of a tight spot. Starting as an informal handyman at the motel, and soon proving more than handy, within a few weeks Ernie had installed himself in Vivian's bedroom at the Blackburn manse. But who exactly the victim was in this sordid pas de deux remains an open question.

When Annie was finally released from the hospital, she returned home to find that Ernie Niles had in every way taken Roland's place. Shortly thereafter, Vivian married Ernie, acquiring her third husband in less than five years. Although larcenous by nature, the feckless Niles was nothing like the predator Blackburn had been, and by all accounts he treated Annie with far more kindness than her mother did. The week after their wedding, Annie hastily returned to her Catholic school in Kennewick, and the following spring she graduated with honors.

Reluctant to return home, and still too fragile to deal with the rigors of independent living at college, Annie made a somewhat impulsive decision to take vows and enter the convent adjacent to her school as a postulant in its spiritual order. While her mother seemed to welcome the decision—it kept Annie out of her hair—Norma did not initially approve of the decision. She declined to intervene, however, ultimately deciding it was in Annie's best interest to let her make her own decision. A few years down the road, as Norma suspected might happen, Annie's growing second thoughts about committing the rest of her life to the Church led her to depart the convent before formally taking full vows. Now in her early twenties, and much stronger emotionally and mentally than she'd been in a decade, Annie, at Norma's invitation, temporarily moved to Twin Peaks to be closer to her sister as she navigated the difficult transition back to civilian life. Norma put her to work as a waitress at the Double R, where Annie seemed to fit right in, and with Vivian and Ernie out of sight and mind, her life finally appeared to be on a healthy track.

Shortly before Annie moved in with Norma, another event of note occurred: Vivian Smythe Niles and husband Ernie arrived in Twin Peaks, unannounced, for a visit, ostensibly so that Vivian could introduce her new husband to Norma. The ever polite and fiercely private Norma introduced Vivian to friends and acquaintances as her mother, declining to elaborate on the twisted circumstances that had brought the woman—who had, all too briefly, been her stepmother—into her life. A classic case of emotional sabotage ensued.

While living off her late husband's insurance money, Vivian—who fancied herself an expert on most things—had moved to Seattle with Ernie and invested in an area restaurant, which quickly failed. Vivian's attitude toward Norma's blue-collar Double R—which was, is, and remains a first-rate iteration of the quintessential small-town American eatery—remained snobby and condescending at best. (It was also, on the face of it, a vivid reminder to Vivian of Marty's and her own working-class origins, which, rather than a source of pride, she saw only as shameful.) Vivian proceeded to backstab Norma, with a twist of the knife that lapped her previous offenses as an evil fairy-tale stepmother by a country mile. Ahead of their visit, she published an anonymous tip in the local newspaper that a secretive and prominent travel writer and food critic—by the name of M. T. Wentz—would soon be visiting the Double R. Norma, in anticipation of this anonymous visit, brightened up the diner—tablecloths, floral arrangements, candles, etc.—and added some special items to the menu. While Vivian was still in town, M. T. Wentz's review appeared in print—a scathing and condescending dismissal of the entire Double R enterprise. By all accounts, Norma was emotionally devastated. Vivian then proceeded to take particular delight in revealing to Norma that she was the author of the article. Furious, Norma finally told the woman who had engineered so much of the misery in her family's life where to go and how to get there. They never spoke to each other again.

As vicious as Vivian's assault against Norma and her restaurant seemed, she may well have been playing a secondary angle while visiting Twin Peaks.

Ernie Niles had always fancied himself a clever and resilient con, but once he entered the ring with Vivian Smythe Lindstrom Blackburn, he was way outside his weight class. It would have taken Vivian very little effort to discover that her dear Ernie had, in the not-too-distant past, done a stretch for fraud in the Washington State Penitentiary that coincided with time served by one Hank Jennings—for vehicular manslaughter, a crime committed as an accomplice of Josie Packard in her failed murder attempt of Andrew Packard—also known as Norma's husband. Vivian also had to have known that her appearance at the diner with Ernie "the Professor" Niles—as he was known inside the joint—would kick up sparks of recognition with Hank and, knowing how elastic Ernie's moral controls were, nothing good would come of it. Predictably, none did.

Within days, Hank had embroiled Ernie in a get-rich-quick scheme, running drugs across the Canadian border for his old crime associates, the Renault family—an easy-money offer that Ernie, predictably, could not refuse. Upon returning from their initial trip to set up the deal, Ernie found himself a pawn in another game when he was flipped by DEA agent Denise Bryson—her possession of surveillance photos of Ernie with known criminals and felons, clearly in violation of his parole terms, did the trick. In exchange for immunity from prosecution, Ernie agreed to front a subsequent sting operation run by Bryson and Special Agent Dale Cooper to take down the Renaults.

Niles wore a wire the next day to an arranged "buy" at a run-down rural location called Dead Dog Farm, resulting in near disaster. Ernie's heavy perspiration under pressure disabled the microphone, and the smoke that leaked from his shirt nearly blew the deal. Only the cool, quick-thinking, and collected reactions of Agents Cooper and Bryson prevented the sting from going sideways; a net dropped on the principals, and the Renaults' stateside operations were permanently crippled. Hank Jennings, swept up in the melee as an accomplice, had spent his last days as a free man and was soon returned to the state pen for a twenty-five-year stretch. As previously noted in the Briggs dossier, only two years later he would die at the hands of a convict with family connections to the Renaults. It's an ill wind, etc., but the upshot was that Norma Jennings was finally freed from her lamentable spouse. (More on how that affected her personal life to come.)

For his cooperation with the authorities, Ernie Niles, as promised, was free to go. Grateful he had dodged disaster, a bigger surprise awaited him when he returned home to Seattle, where Vivian—having left Twin Peaks earlier, after her final confrontation with Norma—had arranged a special greeting. Ernie found all his belongings packed and stacked outside the gated drive of their Seattle home, in the pouring rain, at which point a process server slapped him with divorce papers Vivian had prepared.

So, it leads one to wonder, had Vivian, from the start, planned their visit to Twin Peaks as a way to neatly shed a suddenly inconvenient husband? If so, was her deliberate attack against Norma's self-esteem simply the cherry on top of that sundae? Or was she a multitasking monster who had simply planned to clip the wings of both of these birds with one stone? Either way, the chilling glimpse into this woman's pathological indifference to every person around her makes your blood run cold. And the full extent of the damage she'd done wasn't even accounted for yet.

With his marriage to Vivian, Ernie Niles, middle-aged grifter, reached his personal and professional high-water mark. From the moment of his abject dismissal, the rest of Ernie's life traced a slow, predictable downhill slide to the grave: arrests, convictions, time served, bankruptcy, poverty, alcoholism, homelessness, and a solitary, neglected death in the waiting room of a Pierce County hospital in 2005, his ashes scattered over Puget Sound by a prison charity organization. Exit Ernie Niles. (I know we're trained to withhold our sympathy from the inveterately criminal, Chief, but I have to confess I find myself feeling something stubbornly like sympathy for the weak-minded, rudderless Ernie. Drifting through life like a dandelion on a foul breeze, dying alone in abject poverty—I'd still prefer his company over that of his brutal ex every time.)

Speaking of whom, Vivian Smythe Lindstrom Blackburn Niles snagged one last husband within a year, a retired insurance executive from Bellevue who fancied the cut of her jib. Vivian had at last convinced a member of the class she'd so desperately aspired to join that she belonged in its marbled, Italianate halls. I truly wish I could report that some version of karmic comeuppance at last paid this human wrecking ball a visit, but, circumstantially, at least, no such evidence is in view. Husband number four—Simon Halliwell was the poor man's name—passed through the pearly gates in 2009, after choking on a stubborn chunk of cruise ship filet mignon somewhere between Athens and Positano. The widow Halliwell accompanied her husband's body home and installed him in the family vault, outside Seattle. Vivian was finally left wealthy, secure, and alone, and she seemed to prefer it that way. No more husbands. No more victims. The next time she got her name in the papers was when, after a brief, unspecified illness, she died in 2013 and joined Mr. Halliwell in his mausoleum.

I'd like to think she suffered, felt remorse, or paid some kind of price—deep down inside—for the ragged and roughshod way she ran over every person who crossed her path in life. We'll never know. Maybe living the way that she did, incapable of love, joy, deep feeling, or even affection, was punishment enough. Maybe life was all a torment to her, no more than a form of mere existing, not *living*. It would also be easy to assume that, at some point in her life—details of her early years remain hidden in dense fog, impossible now to retrieve—she herself had been hurt or victimized in some way that crippled her inside, an injury she simply felt compelled to pass along. We'll never know that, either. If that's not the case, the temptation with Vivian Smith is to conclude that some people are simply born bad, that the path they walk is fated as dark and evil, and woe betide all those who encounter them along the way. Why do the wicked attract us so? What hint of glamour, hope for material gain, or assumption of fleeting happiness do they radiate, that we can find ourselves so easily, fatally taken in? I confess I do not understand this impulse, Chief—not so much that of the criminal at heart (after all, they may be acting with no more forethought than a lion that instinctively shreds the throat of its next meal) as that of the willing victims who line up for the chance to show these monsters their neck. Are we just trapped in an endless loop of some inescapable ecosystem, predators and prey, feeding, dying, and fading away to make room for the next round of actors? What possible bloody purpose could such a miserable cycle serve? What's our takeaway?

(Forgive the philosophizing. I know it's our job to keep these predators at bay, to stand between them and their victims. I embrace that role with solemn obligation, but every once in a while the banality of this endless carnage makes me want to scream.)

My anger persists here because of the damage done to her daughters. One more than the other. For Annie Blackburn's fate, Vivian Smith deserves a special place in hell, and if she didn't suffer it here, I hope she's found it in whatever existence awaits beyond.

INITIAL TP    DATE 9 / 6 / 17

FEDERAL BUREAU OF INVESTIGATION

CASE #    008-072-0119          BUREAU FILE #    TP-07/18

# ANNIE BLACKBURN

PRESTON, Tamara

CASE AGENT        *TP*

INITIAL

# CONFIDENTIAL

FIELD OFFICE CRIMINAL INVESTIGATIVE
AND ADMINISTRATIVE FILES

See also Nos.   77-18-4500

6787

35312

FEDERAL BUREAU
OF INVESTIGATION

*Field Office Criminal Investigative
and Administrative Files*

I like to think she found her own fleeting happiness in those few weeks she spent at the Double R: her sister's unconditional love, the support of a community of friends who genuinely liked her for her charm, intelligence, and beauty. A belated introduction to the kind of world she so wanted to know and deserved to live in. She apparently also experienced a chance to develop the first serious romantic relationship of her adult life, as you know, with none other than your old friend Special Agent Dale Cooper.

As I think about what happened to her subsequently, a temptation rises within me to in some way hold Agent Cooper responsible. There's a long chain of circumstance here that threads back to the worst—self-admitted—mistake of Cooper's life. I'm alluding, as I'm sure you know, to his youthful dalliance with the wife of his ex-partner and former mentor, Windom Earle. We know now that Caroline Earle suffered such extreme mental and emotional distress during the course of her marriage that her reaching out to Cooper as she did seems likely to have been a cry for help more than an attempt to seduce. Cooper never could resist a bird with a broken wing—you know as well as I do by now that it's a central part of his makeup: white knight syndrome, the irresistible urge to rescue every damsel in distress he came across.

(Without stepping too far into profiling here, my feeling is that this relates directly to Cooper's troubled relationship with his own mother, a fragile woman who suffered through a sizable portion of Cooper's teenage years in varying degrees of mental and physical suffering—the product of her own turbulent marriage. Before she eventually straightened herself out, Cooper spent a lot of time tending to her, taking care of her—perhaps too much time—and this seems to have encouraged in him a moral conviction, if not an obligation toward "saving" women in jeopardy that he carried into his own adulthood.)

CLASSIFICATION    CONFIDENTIAL

Although Cooper's relationship with Caroline stayed focused on emotional support and remained, for 99 percent of its duration, platonic, the one moment it crossed over into physical consummation happened to coincide with Windom Earle snapping his strings. This is what we know:

# FEDERAL BUREAU OF INVESTIGATION

CASE # 008-072-0119          BUREAU FILE # TP-08/18

# WINDOM EARLE

PRESTON, Tamara

CASE AGENT          *TP*

INITIAL

# CONFIDENTIAL

FIELD OFFICE CRIMINAL INVESTIGATIVE
AND ADMINISTRATIVE FILES

See also Nos. 001-43-25

6787

2663

As a young man, Windom Earle was, by any definition, a prodigiously talented individual. A chess grandmaster by fourteen, admitted to the University of Pennsylvania at sixteen, a graduate at eighteen, Earle obtained a master's in criminal justice at Penn State and then applied to and was accepted by the Bureau as a trainee. (On his application, he cites having seen, at the age of ten, the popular 1951 film *I Was a Communist for the F.B.I.* as the pivotal inspiration for his law enforcement career.)

After he completed training at Quantico with historically high marks, Earle's first field assignment came in the mid-sixties, as a liaison and security officer between the Bureau and evolving elements of what had long been known as Project Blue Book, during which time we now know he crossed paths with Douglas Milford. (His subsequent partnership with you, Chief, as a founding member of the Bureau's Blue Rose group, needs, I'm sure, no detailing here.) In 1973, while serving as a Bureau investigator in the Watergate hearing, Earle met and began dating Caroline Wickam, a young law student who was working on the staff of chief prosecutor Samuel Dash. They married, in a civil ceremony in Washington, D.C., on August 10, 1974, the day after Nixon resigned from office.

By the early eighties, although he continued to work out of the Bureau's Philadelphia office, Earle and Caroline lived in Pittsburgh, her hometown, where Caroline was now a partner in a thriving corporate law practice. Earle commuted back and forth, usually once or twice a week. They'd been married for ten years and had no children—Caroline was fiercely committed to her career, an apparent point of strain between them—when Earle began working with the next of your protégés to join the Philadelphia office, Dale Cooper.

First, a disclaimer: Elements of this narrative may be familiar to you from a review of Cooper's own words on the subject culled from his daily tapes to Diane, or rather from Diane's transcripts of the tapes. After an independent survey of all the available facts, I have concluded that the tapes/transcripts have been heavily redacted and modified—it's safe to say that "Diane's" motivations for doing so, at this point, are well known to us—and cannot be considered a consistently reliable source.

In the early 1980s, an investigation into a murder by a potential serial killer—which we now have strong reason to suspect was a series of killings committed by Earle himself—brought young agent Cooper to the Pittsburgh Bureau office for his first field assignment. He was soon tasked to participate in the ongoing investigation of these murders, an effort spearheaded early on by Agent Earle. We also know that Earle suspected that a mutual attraction existed between Cooper and Caroline from the moment he introduced them to each other at a Bureau Christmas party in Philadelphia the previous year. Cooper himself admitted to the attraction in his tapes, but it's unlikely anything would have come of it had the months he spent in Pittsburgh working on this case not ensued. Although his native brilliance managed to conceal it from everyone in his life, from statements he made later while in custody, we also know there's ample reason to suspect that by this point Windom Earle was already far down the road toward losing his mind.

So Earle not only suspected his wife and partner's budding affinity; he perversely proceeded to do everything in his power to push them together in order to prove that it existed, thereby justifying the repellent response he was already formulating. Finding frequent excuses to work out of town, ostensibly on trips related to their ongoing investigation, Earle in fact remained in town, undercover, in order to conduct covert surveillance. He even took steps to nudge them toward each other—for example, anonymously drawing them both to the same location so they would meet "coincidentally"—acting as a deranged, vengeful Cupid. This culminated in the one ill-fated weekend they would spend as lovers, when Earle crossed the threshold from private madman to public murderer.

While the attack appeared to be a classic "crime of passion"—apparently his intention and, perhaps, what he hoped would become the foundation of his legal defense—Windom Earle didn't count on the fact that Agent Cooper had by this time privately realized that Earle himself was the serial killer they had been chasing all along. Caroline, it seems, reached this same conclusion, also on her own, and confirmed it when she and Cooper finally examined the facts together. It's now clear that when Earle took his wife's life and nearly finished Cooper's, he was acting to prevent their revealing his guilt to the Bureau. At which point this "crime of passion" became a convenient cover for our purposes, as well as his, to conceal the far uglier truth. A trial was avoided, and the truth was buried with Caroline. Either interpretation would have been more than enough to justify Earle's confinement in a secure facility for the criminally insane, an entirely appropriate outcome. This tragedy, I also now realize, became the means through which you yourself met Agent Cooper, who in every way lived up to the hopes and ideals Windom Earle had once embodied, and so bitterly betrayed.

The level of Cooper's suffering and remorse in the terrible aftermath of these tragic events can't be underestimated. He fiercely committed himself to counseling and self-reflection during his physical recovery in a way that was 100 percent sincere. He's on record—well, tape, anyway—confirming that this experience represented the most difficult lesson of his life, and, admirably, he took it to heart. But that's not quite the same thing as entirely purging an ingrained impulse to save a troubled woman from herself, is it, Chief?

(Am I being too harsh on Agent Cooper here? I'm open to suggestions, so please let me know if you feel that's the case. Notwithstanding its importance, I believe Cooper's obsession with the Laura Palmer case harbors echoes of this tendency.)

So let me bring this home: Was this established trait a factor in Cooper's attraction to Annie Blackburn? It's possible that what drew him to Annie was something much purer and simpler: the fact that they'd both endured—and survived—vicious assaults by dangerous criminals against the core of their being, which nearly cost them their lives. That such a powerful personal narrative connected them shouldn't be minimized. For all we know, had their relationship been given a chance to grow, it could have become the most healing bond either of them had ever experienced, possibly even (a heartbreaking thought) the love of a lifetime. It's not out of the question, and I know it must be the least of what you would have wished for your friend. Sadly, we'll never know.

We do know that after nearly ten years in solitary lockdown at a federal max-security facility, Earle engineered a breathtakingly daring escape and vanished without a trace. We also know that, in the kind of perverse defiance he relished, he retreated to a hideout he'd previously established in the abandoned Eastern State Penitentiary, in Philadelphia, the nation's oldest and most notorious prison for the criminally insane. From there he launched the plot for revenge he'd apparently been planning all this time.

BUREAU FILE #

TP-08 / 18

DIVISION

PHL / PA

INITIAL _TP_  DATE 9 / 6 / 17

# FEDERAL BUREAU OF INVESTIGATION

CASE #    008-072-0119        BUREAU FILE #    TP-09/18

# BACK IN
# TWIN PEAKS

PRESTON, Tamara

**CASE AGENT**

_TP_

INITIAL

# CONFIDENTIAL

FIELD OFFICE CRIMINAL INVESTIGATIVE
AND ADMINISTRATIVE FILES

See also Nos. 001-274-4

6787

2663
94-63-66

*Field Office Criminal Investigative*
*and Administrative Files*

Earle had been in Twin Peaks for more than a month—his crime spree of murders and misdemeanors are well known to us and need not be reviewed here—when Norma and other friends at the Double R encouraged Annie Blackburn to enter a local beauty contest, the Miss Twin Peaks pageant. With typically earnest sincerity, Annie wrote a speech, which she gave in the "talent competition," that employed standard homilies about world peace, quoted Chief Seattle, wowed the judges—a low bar, admittedly—and won the crown. At which point all hell broke loose: Under the cover of pyrotechnic distractions, Windom Earle kidnapped Annie and made off with her undetected. The trail grows hazy from this point forward.

Earle took her to a—still to this day—undiscovered location, somewhere in the Ghostwood National Forest. (Hints of a "supernatural" angle creep in here, which I'm not inclined to credit, but the Archivist's and our own subsequent experiences with the Cooper case may justify a revisiting.) Earle's objective seems crystal clear: With Annie in hand, he hoped to draw Cooper to him and finish the job he'd begun in Pittsburgh years earlier. Later that same night, Cooper, accompanied by two members of the Sheriff's Department, traveled to a place in the woods where he apparently had reason to believe Earle might be holding her. Cooper "went in alone"—this according to Sheriff Truman's account—and then "disappeared" overnight.

The difficulty is: I don't know what he meant by either description. Went in where? Disappeared how? There's no elaboration, and Truman has ever since remained tight-lipped about it, out of, I suppose, unswerving loyalty to his friend. But Cooper's location and what happened to him over the next twelve hours remain stubbornly in the dark. The next morning, near dawn, Sheriff Truman and one of his deputies found Cooper and Annie in a nearby clearing. Deputies rushed Annie to a hospital. They took Cooper back to his room at the Great Northern, where Doc Hayward checked him out and pronounced him

healthy but in need of rest, and Cooper spent the remainder of that day recovering at the hotel.

Windom Earle was never seen again. No trace of him, dead or alive, ever turned up in those woods or elsewhere. As you know, within a few days Cooper himself disappeared not only from Twin Peaks but from every map or grid in the Bureau's tool kit for twenty-five years.

Annie Blackburn spent one day in the hospital, during which she appeared relatively unaffected by whatever ordeal she'd endured and claimed to have no memories of it. The next morning, hospital staff found her in an abject catatonic state. Eyes open, staring straight ahead, unseeing, pupils fixed, completely unresponsive to any visual or aural stimuli. Mystified, they could find no underlying physical explanation; her vitals were robust. She remained this way for the next ten days, during which they treated her with intravenous fluids and nutrition and all her vitals remained strong. At every moment, Norma or one of her friends from the diner attended her bedside. Annie's condition slowly improved, to the point that, with assistance, she was eventually able to sit up and walk around. Her affect remained passive and compliant—serene, even—throughout. She allowed nursing staff to dress, feed, and bathe her as needed. But she never spoke again, never acknowledged anyone else's presence, never even appeared to see or hear anyone or anything in front of her.

Two months on, Norma moved Annie back home, where she began to take care of her personally. (Knowing Norma, this hardly comes as a surprise, whereas their mother, Vivian, never even returned Norma's calls about Annie's condition—she'd already moved on to the next husband, where no mention of her past was welcome.) One year to the day after Annie had been found in the woods, Norma came home to find her slumped in bed, in a pool of her own blood; she'd slit her wrists again with the shards of a shattered glass. Norma discovered her just in time and rushed her to the hospital. Once again, Annie never gave the slightest indication that she knew what she'd done to herself, where she was, or whom she was with. She remained awake and alert and completely detached from her surroundings. She did, however, speak one sentence the next morning in the hospital. As far as anyone could remember, it was the only thing she'd said since the day they found her in the woods. Although there were people in the room, including Norma, no one there had spoken to her—they knew better—so she wasn't responding to a question asked by anyone present.

"I'm fine," she said.

They noted this on her chart: 8:38 A.M. After which, according to their records, Annie lapsed back into her impenetrable isolation and did not utter another word. The doctor on call noted this on her chart: "May have been responding to auditory hallucination."

Annie's condition did not improve. On the recommendation of every doctor she consulted, Norma finally acknowledged that, if she were to have any hope of carrying on the rest of her own working life, she would no longer be able to shoulder full responsibility for her sister's care. After her second suicide attempt, Annie required around-the-clock supervision and observation. Once again, reliably, Annie's mother, Vivian, refused all of Norma's entreaties to help with any aspect of Annie's condition. Within a few weeks, after a community fund-raiser helped Norma meet the burdensome financial commitment—Ben Horne, somewhat surprisingly, was a major contributor—Annie was transferred to a private psychiatric hospital near Spokane.

She's been there ever since. I visited the hospital recently and spent more than two hours sitting with her. She's still quite beautiful, her face unlined and youthful in appearance, peaceful in temperament, and blissfully detached from everything and everyone around her. She looks as if she's hardly aged a day. She sits alone and still every day, all day, without any need for or interest in external stimulation or activity. Compliant and cooperative, she shows no interest in feeding herself, but never objects to being fed. Her eyes, far from appearing dull and vacant—as her condition and diagnosis would lead you to expect—seem alive, filled by a vivid and mysterious internal life. But one last anomaly jumped out at me as I examined her records and video files, and it may interest you as well, Chief.

Every year, once a year, on the anniversary of that day she was found in the woods, without prompting or responding to any inquiry directed to her, at precisely 8:38 in the morning, she speaks that same single sentence to no one in particular.

"I'm fine," she says.

That's the only identifiable feature I can find in an otherwise flat and featureless landscape. The doctors tell me that now, a quarter of a century on, it's highly doubtful her condition will ever change or improve.

And so it seems, with an endless ellipsis rather than a period, here is where we take our leave of the lamentable life's journey of Annie Blackburn.

INITIAL *TP*  DATE 9/6/17

**FEDERAL BUREAU OF INVESTIGATION**

CASE #  008-072-0119   BUREAU FILE #  TP-10/18

# MISS TWIN PEAKS

PRESTON, Tamara

CASE AGENT

INITIAL

# CONFIDENTIAL

FIELD OFFICE CRIMINAL INVESTIGATIVE
AND ADMINISTRATIVE FILES

See also Nos.  94-63-66
2663
8818

FEDERAL BUREAU
OF INVESTIGATION

*Field Office Criminal Investigative
and Administrative Files*

SUBJECT

MISS TWIN PEAKS

10

I want to include one curious and, perhaps, related postscript. In the aftermath of Windom Earle's one-man crime spree, life in Twin Peaks took a considerable amount of time to return to "normal." This detail stood out for me:

You'll recall from Major Briggs's dossier the story of Lana Budding Milford, the young sexual adventuress who was—for a night, anyway—married to the late Doug Milford, publisher of the *Twin Peaks Post* and erstwhile lifelong spook. When Annie Blackburn disappeared, reappeared, and quickly thereafter descended into her twilight state, the organizers of the pageant—after observing a respectable sixty-day interval—made an official public announcement that their elected representative would be unable to fulfill the appointed functions of her office. And, yes, as a civic position, Miss Twin Peaks does serve verifiable, if hardly profound, small-town public relations duties, along the lines of ribbon cuttings, high school homecoming games, and photo ops with visiting dignitaries.

The town council voted that, in Annie's tragic absence, the Miss Twin Peaks runner-up would assume the title and fill the position. That was, according to the scorecards, Lana Budding Milford. The fact that in the weeks following her husband's untimely death Lana was seen—at various times in various locations by a number of different witnesses—canoodling with Doug's surviving brother, the town's longtime mayor Dwayne Milford, should not be viewed as a persuasive or prejudicial factor in their decision, or so I was encouraged to believe. Comforting her elderly brother-in-law in his time of need was viewed, more charitably, as a natural expression of Lana's ripe and abundant compassion for her fellow man. Ahem.

Although the eternal appeal of the "dark feminine" archetype continues to fascinate, that's not the detail that interests me here, however. I came across an inventory of Doug's possessions at the time of his death, as an addendum to the autopsy, briefly summarized here:

- Cause of death: cardiac arrest.
- Body unclothed, found in bed.

(The morning after, you'll recall, Doug and Lana's wedding night in the Honeymoon Suite of the Great Northern Hotel.)

- Personal accessories recovered: on the decedent's bedside table, one Rolex watch, one jade green ring.

Okay. The wedding had taken place approximately fourteen hours earlier. The bride and groom had been observed, as tradition dictates, exchanging rings during the recital of their vows by a roomful of witnesses. I looked into this. Although the ceremony is more than twenty-five years removed, not one of the fifteen or so attendees I interviewed recalls the ring that Lana gave to Doug as a "jade green ring," but instead identified it as a conventional unadorned gold wedding band. I had this confirmed by the town jeweler, still in business, who was able to provide a receipt showing that Doug Milford himself had bought both his and his wife's bands a few days before the nuptials.

When I inquired as to the disposition of the "jade green ring" postmortem, I was told that, per department protocol, it would have been returned to the widow Milford.

(To refresh your memory, there is a thread running throughout the dossier about an appearing and, apparently, disappearing "green ring." It's mentioned a number of times, as early as the papers of Meriwether Lewis and as late as the Nixon White House, where Doug Milford himself may have observed it on the left hand of the troubled late president. The wearer is more than a few times described as "worrying" the ring, twisting it on his or her finger, and, more often than not, its appearance presages impending peril, misfortune, or untimely death. I confess I do not know what to make of this at all and wonder if you do.)

Lana, as previously noted, lingered in Twin Peaks just long enough after Doug's demise for probate to certify the conditions of the will, at which point she quickly split the scene on the wings of a multimillion-dollar windfall. She shows up next in the Hamptons, on the arms of an ascending line of decorative male escorts, until she snags a hedge fund manager well on his way to banking his first billion. (Remember, this was the mid-nineties, when *authentic* New York City billionaires remained a genuinely rare breed.)

On her way up the plutocratic food chain, Lana briefly dated a notorious resident of a certain eponymous tower on Fifth Avenue, who was either between wives, stepping out, or merely window-shopping. I was able to locate one society-page photograph of the duo at some charity gala, in which the man appears to be wearing an unusual green ring on his left ring finger, but the resolution of the shot proved insufficient for closer examination. In any case, their relationship was short-lived. As this was near the nadir of the man's whizbang financial exploits—rife with bankruptcies, noxious litigations, and other related derring-do—one suspects that the ever resourceful Lana may have managed to finagle a peek at the man's bottom line and decided she should chum neighboring waters for bigger fish. Gee, wonder what ever happened to that guy.

The man she eventually married, by the way, bested Doug Milford's matrimonial stamina by a substantial margin, as the happy couple lived in wedded bliss all the way until 2008, when the mogul dropped dead of a heart attack in Antigua—the location of their "winter palace"—during his morning jog on the beach. Once again, the widow Lana made out like a bandit. I hear tell she then drifted toward the South of France, but at that point I lost track of the woman— or, should I say, interest. As a kindred spiritual cousin to Vivian Smith, her story lacks the edifying moral fiber I prefer in my cautionary tales. Lana certainly had amassed enough bank by this point to call it a day, and, to put it kindly, with regard to her preferred line of work, the engine was still running, but the chassis needed an overhaul.

Anyway, who cares? As my mother used to say, trash is trash even if it's in a Tiffany bag.

INITIAL *TP*  DATE 9 / 6 / 17

# FEDERAL BUREAU OF INVESTIGATION

CASE # 008-072-0119

BUREAU FILE # TP-11/18

# DR. LAWRENCE JACOBY

PRESTON, Tamara

CASE AGENT

INITIAL

# CONFIDENTIAL

FIELD OFFICE CRIMINAL INVESTIGATIVE
AND ADMINISTRATIVE FILES

See also Nos. 42-1642-32

8818

5411-08

1719

SUBJECT

DR. LAWRENCE JACOBY

11

BUREAU FILE #

TP-11/18

DIVISION

PHL/PA

FEDERAL BUREAU
OF INVESTIGATION

*Field Office Criminal Investigative
and Administrative Files*

You'll recall that when the dossier last dealt with Dr. Jacoby—the town's free-stylin' New Age psychiatrist—he had just been informed by the Washington State medical board that, for his full twenty-four-hour diner menu of ethical code violations, his license to practice medicine had been summarily revoked. Awaiting judgment, Jacoby then repaired to his childhood home on the Hawaiian island of Kauai. Living off savings—and a tidy sum left to him by his recently departed brother Robert—he spent the next two years in Hanalei Bay, gone to ground, licking his wounds and searching for a way to reinvent himself.

While he could no longer legally hang up a shingle, the good doctor showed no inclination to abandon his well-trodden path dancing along the margins on the outer precincts of reality's most radical possibilities. Jacoby threw himself into field studies with Hawaiian shamans and alternative medicines, which he chronicled in an early online blog, which we'd call it today. A substantial chunk of this content focused on the ways of the menehune, the folkloric "little people" of native South Sea Islander culture. Akin to similar mythologies in many other aboriginal traditions—leprechauns, pixies, elves, et al.—the menehune are usually depicted as mischievous nature spirits and master builders of various inexplicable engineering projects, usually involving stone and water. I'll spare you most of the colorful details, Chief, but on more than one occasion Jacoby claims to have made contact with the little folk, who revealed to him that they're not of earthly origin and that their mission here on earth is to help steer the "newer root race of human beings" away from our unfortunate genetic propensity for violence and self-destruction. Setting aside for a moment the efficacy of their "mission," if we judge these wee folk solely on the degree to which they've succeeded in this regard, they're running well below standards we apply to basic government work.

Jacoby also mentions a competing theory—more archaeology-based than mystical—that these little people may simply hail from an earlier race of smaller humanoid bipeds—as in "pygmies"—who settled the isolated island chain some eons before the migratory Polynesians showed up in their outriggers. He also offers that this doesn't in any way rule out the possibility that the little people were alien in origin to begin with, putting us right back where we started.

(UFOs and "the grays" make a brief appearance here as well, which gave me the giggles one night, after two glasses of wine, when I found myself picturing them in grass skirts.)

Anyway, you get the drift. And at the least, I think this now gives us a reasonable working hypothesis for the basis of Jacoby's enduring bond with his old friend Jerry Horne: killer weed. (To which I now feel compelled to reiterate that Jacoby lived in Hanalei Bay, first made famous as the home of Puff the Magic Dragon.)

As the Internet mushroomed, Jacoby's blog gradually brought him back to some fraction of his previous 1960s notoriety, and to the attention of many prominent counterculture figures who had through the years kept, as they like to say, "on truckin." At the personal invitation of an unspecified band member, Jacoby spent most of 1994–95 on the road with the Grateful Dead, or, as I once heard Albert refer to them, "the world's greatest bad garage band." (Did you know Albert is a stereo and vinyl enthusiast with a jazz collection that numbers in the thousands? Yes, you probably did.) Whether Jacoby served the band as a "senior spiritual adviser"—the doctor's version of his job description—or, according to one ex-roadie's more blunt assessment, "the Banzai Pipeline to all manner of psychotropic traveling," Jacoby's time on the bus came to an abrupt end with the untimely death of singer and lead guitarist Jerry Garcia. I believe that Jacoby's enduring fondness for loud and colorful neckties is most likely a tribute to his old friend.

Jacoby's peripatetic ways continued; he next turns up as a "resident fellow" with a sketchy progressive think tank in Amsterdam called the Zonderkop Institute—which translates as "Born Without a Head." The organization itself, however, was born with a head: It was founded in 1981 by one Dr. Jost Poepjes— which translates, and I'm not making this up, as "Doctor Little Poops." According to its website, the Institute's mission statement claims it is dedicated to—this is my own slightly rougher translation—"finding alternative ways of raising human consciousness, and fast, before we blow all this shit up." The Institute's address places it directly upstairs from a popular hashish bar owned, I'm guessing not coincidentally, by Dr. Little Poops himself.

(I have come across a theory explaining this weird Dutch last-name business, although it may be of interest only to me: Holland was occupied by Napoleonic France for a short period at the turn of the eighteenth century, during which time the French instituted the country's first comprehensive census. It seems many of their unhappy Dutch subjects may have offered ridiculous and, to the non-Dutch-speaking French bureaucrats tallying the count, untranslatable surnames as a mild form of protest—for example, the wildly popular surname Niemands, which means "Nobody." In the end, the joke fell more heavily on the Dutch after Napoleon met his Waterloo and the French split the lowland scene but left the goofy names behind.)

Dr. Jacoby's own two-year stay in Amsterdam came to an end in 1998, when Dr. Little Poops decided that the impending—and, it turned out, entirely media-driven—Y2K crisis signaled the "end of civilization as we know it." Along with a few die-hard followers, Dr. LP repaired to a "secure and unspecified ecological biosphere in the far north of Sweden" to hunker down during the apocalypse. (And there Dr. Little Poops vanishes from the radar screen of history.) Jacoby did not attend.

Taking this millennial setback in stride, Dr. Jacoby returned stateside and headed straight for Florida, where he pitched in as a volunteer during the "hanging chad" portion of the 2000 presidential election recount. He spent whatever free time this gig allowed by offering "lay counsel" to distraught/defensive former Ralph Nader supporters. Although no longer able to work as a licensed physician, due to his loss of credentials, Jacoby released a noteworthy lay paper on his findings online, identifying what he called the "defiant liberal denial syndrome." The article got some play in a few progressive media outlets and helped persuade Jacoby that it might be time to turn his still formidable power of mind toward political activism.

His decision was reinforced less than a year later: Jacoby happened to be in NYC on 9/11, participating in an anthropological conference on shamanism at the Museum of Natural History. In the days that followed, during countless hours of volunteer work that he spent comforting the wounded and traumatized, he came to view the terrorist attack through the eternal lens of cause and effect—or, to state it more simply, karma—and interpreted it as the first toll of the bell striking midnight for the American Experiment. He predicted, correctly and with no evident glee, that the government would overreact, lash out at the wrong targets, and kick off an even more destructive cycle of cause/effect that would only make the emerging global crises worse. When the search for weapons of mass destruction came up empty, kicking the legs out from under the administration's rationale for invading Iraq, Jacoby took no pleasure in learning that his instincts had been confirmed. He interpreted this as confirmation of his theory that the United States, and perhaps the world, might be entering into what he saw as a "Kali Yuga"—an ancient Hindu term for a "dark age." In 2003, on the wings of that vision, he decided it was time to head back home to Twin Peaks.

The purpose of this second return was not to reengage with the community he'd abandoned—and, in truth, felt abandoned by—more than ten years earlier. Instead Jacoby bought a used mobile home and hauled it up to a remote hardscrabble acre that he bought for peanuts near the peak of White Tail Mountain. Once he'd set up shop, he began making supply runs into town—at most, once a week, and usually after dark. The only person in the area I can verify he reached out to directly was his old "bud" Jerry Horne, who I believe became the first and only outside financial contributor to Jacoby's new enterprise. Lawrence Jacoby evidenced zero interest in reliving any part of his former life in Twin Peaks; he had embarked on a new mission now, a vision fueled by rededication to his youthful sixties-era radicalism.

He dedicated the next year to educating himself about all the advantages the Internet now offered as a means of distribution for his idiosyncratic messianic vision. During this period, he carefully crafted a new persona for himself to serve as the herald of that message, a character he called Dr. Amp.

In 2006, just after he turned seventy, Jacoby launched the first live episodes of what he predicted would become his "Internet media empire," and *The Dr. Amp Blast* made its debut, streaming live, one hour a night, five nights a week. Although the early editions vary wildly in quality—he made them all available online after each live stream, as some of the first "podcasts"—his message and tone remained remarkably consistent: Dr. Amp offered a ferocious running critique against a world turning mad, a commonsense prophet offering a nightly jeremiad that railed against the ignorant, the privileged, and the false. He remained a true believer in medicine and the scientific method—tie-dyed, of course, with his sixties New Ageism—preaching truth against what he described as the rising forces of corporatism, the corruption of wealth inequality, and the corrosive effects of what he called "cannibal capitalism" on the human mind, body, and spirit. Dr. Amp not only tossed out political perspectives amid a regular diet of crackpot conspiracy theories, but he offered up practical home remedies to counteract their negative effects: alternative medicines, herbal supplements, ancient methods of meditation and spiritual renewal.

Jacoby had done his homework. Dr. Amp's nightly crusades quickly struck a chord and garnered a small but intensely loyal Internet following. Most of his local listeners from eastern Washington—even including those who'd previously known him in and around Twin Peaks—had no idea where he was broadcasting from or who Dr. Amp actually was. (That changed at least in Twin Peaks, when he began video-streaming his program in 2012.) By 2009, when the economic bubble burst and the big banks nearly went under, plunging the national and global economy into an abyss, Dr. Amp's message of defiant hope, activism, and individual responsibility struck an even more resonant chord. The mystery of Dr. Amp's identity became an indelible part of his mystique, and by 2012 his reputation began to spread beyond the regional, into the national. He refused a few attempts by mainstream media outlets to co-opt his message or seduce him with the idea of reaching a broader audience by waving buckets of cash in his face. He had saved more than enough money over the years to support his modest lifestyle indefinitely and, as he made clear in his very first offering, "as far as people thinking I'm crazy, at my age, I just don't have any fucks left to give."

He did, however, eventually happen onto a unique ancillary revenue stream on his own. In 2015, Dr. Amp began a direct-mail operation after a number of his followers responded to one of his frequent admonitions to "dig yourself out of the shit"—a central theme of his call to self-empowerment, urging people to fight back and seize control of their own lives and destinies. Before long, he added the ideal tool you could use for the job: a (at first) metaphorical "golden shovel" that his followers could visualize to help them complete said task. The desired transformation through undertaking this assignment he described as a process of "intrapersonal alchemy," turning the lead of dull, everyday consciousness into the gold of an evolved human soul, the goal of what he described as a hallowed tradition in esoteric philosophy harking all the way back to the Middle Ages. This led to Jacoby offering literal golden shovels for sale—simple garden spades that he personally spray-painted gold, two coats—in a series of home-crafted commercials, and before long he was selling dozens and eventually hundreds of them a week. Fittingly, he seems to take no interest in using this sideline for personal gain. An examination of his recent tax returns shows that his corporate income grew by 2.5 times, and 90 percent of it he anonymously donated to a variety of charitable progressive causes.

So do we conclude that, through this new identity and means of expression, Dr. Jacoby has "dug himself out of his *own* shit?" I have to add that, while I generally don't find much common ground with either the doctor's complaints or his prescriptions, listening to his show offers some peculiar pleasures; he comes across as a buoyant and likable personality, fueled by righteous indignation, unbound by convention or any shred of need for our approval. Jacoby remains nothing if not a dyed-in-the-wool gadfly, whose synapses appear to fire, more or less coherently, in more directions at once than a daisy cutter.

Lawrence Jacoby is over eighty years old now. There is an air of the tarot's "Magus" about the man—the ancient archetype of a magician who's outlived or conquered the base temptations of life to reach spiritual serenity while still maintaining the height of his powers. As I think of "Dr. Jacoby/Dr. Amp," a character like Prospero comes to mind, a man in the last act of life who's survived the "tempest" of human turmoil and by doing so gained the ability to see beyond its commonplace illusions. A man who lives at one with nature and its pagan "spirits," whose developed senses can now "pierce the veil" of existence and leave him able and willing to share the wisdom one mines from such hard-earned territory. (King Lear would be the tragic version, a privileged man who arrives at the same place through loss and hubris that will eventually cost him his life.) That Jacoby's personal "ground" sits atop a mountain in a remote range in eastern Washington, which, the dossier has established, is as steeped in mystery as any ancient Himalayan peak, seems altogether fitting.

As you may be able to tell, Chief, I'm experiencing a bit of a "What's it all about?" moment with this inquiry. I'd like to believe there's more to life than what we can see or lay our hands on, but the "job" keeps us so focused on the evil that men do that it's a challenge to hold both thoughts at once. My research tells me that people drawn to law enforcement professions, if they're thoughtful at all, perpetually struggle with this conundrum: How do we dig ourselves out of *that* particular shit? I suspect this is part of why you've asked me to take all this on: to instigate the process of confronting that riddle within myself. Is that the secret at the heart of the Blue Rose and the work we do? To identify root causes of human misery and evil, do we first have to find them in ourselves?

A JACOBY P.S.:

Chief, I've found a postscript to Dr. Jacoby's arrival back in Twin Peaks, and it produced an indirect and positive bank-shot consequence to many of the people you know there.

As we learned in the dossier, the hard-luck romance between Ed Hurley and Norma Jennings had over the years run into more impediments than a congressional funding bill. Every time a crack of daylight appeared offering a possibility that they might finally get together, fate slammed the window shut with a steady stream of murders, imprisonments, nervous breakdowns—you name it. The return to incarceration of Hank Jennings seemed to signal the end of this cycle, only to be replaced not long after by the tragedy that befell Annie Blackburn, with Norma devoting herself to her full-time care. Then, no sooner had Annie's worsening condition required permanent around-the-clock hospitalization—another window—than a serious setback in Nadine Hurley's delicate state of mind pulled Ed back into his guilt-ridden caretaker role for her. A year after that, when Nadine finally appeared to be on the mend, and Ed had worked up his courage to break away from his troubled wife once and for all, his nephew James drove his troubled life into a ditch, requiring Ed's help.

When Leland Palmer died in police custody after confessing to the murder of his daughter, Laura, the most innocent of her local boyfriends, a grieving and disillusioned James, took to the open road on his Harley, with no plans to return. Not long afterwards, after being taken in by a predatory older woman outside Portland, Oregon, James stumbled into the role of hapless patsy in a murder scheme straight out of noted noir novelist James M. Cain. (I won't bore you with the details.) Although James narrowly avoided being charged with any crime, he later appeared during trial as a witness for the prosecution. When the highly skilled defense attorney tore his testimony apart—casting serious doubt on James's character, if not his version of events—James felt threatened enough by loose talk about how he could be charged with perjury that he impetuously and unwisely fled town before completing his testimony. A bench warrant was issued to ensure his return. It didn't. We know now that James kept driving all the way to Mexico, where he hid out in Baja, working as a mechanic under an assumed name. The young man didn't have a criminal bone in his body, but trouble sure had a knack for finding him—Major Briggs referred to this in the dossier as something the family has always sarcastically called "Hurley Luck."

James managed to lay low down Mexico way for close to a year, until he got "lucky" again, after repairing the wounded engine block of a Lamborghini Diablo belonging to a Sinaloa Cartel capo. (In the parlance of the aforementioned Cain, the engine was suffering from a bad case of lead poisoning: Someone had opened fire on it with a Schmeisser AR-15 spitting hollow-tip, steel-piercing ordnance.) This cocaine cowboy took such a shine to James's handiwork that he offered him a full-time job at his hillside Jalisco estate, maintaining the hotshot's fleet of seventeen exotic luxury vehicles, another waving red flag the size of Texas that James seems to have missed. About six months later, a rival gang showed up one morning to execute the capo in a hostile takeover—this dog's breakfast involved an undercover sting, crooked cops, and a rogue DEA agent who'd been turned by the cartel. James was one of the shootout's few survivors, having hidden in the trunk of a Rolls, but in the aftermath he was swept up by the federales.

Word of his "indefinite detention" in Mexico eventually found its way back to the Twin Peaks Sheriff's Department. With his friend Sheriff Harry Truman along to help sort things out—and, I've been told, a few helpful calls placed by a certain Deputy Director of the Bureau—a few months later a Mexican judge cleared James of any involvement in the proceedings, and had him escorted to the border, where he was instructed to leave the country and never return. But an immediate return to Twin Peaks wasn't in the cards; that court in Oregon still wanted a pound of flesh from James for fleeing its bench warrant. (His abrupt departure from the trial had not in the end deterred the jury from finding the defendants—Evelyn Marsh and the paramour who had been posing as his brother—guilty as charged of murdering her late husband.)

Attorneys and judges put their heads together and decided that for his sins James owed Oregon six months of his life in minimum security followed by two years' probation, during which time he would not be allowed to leave the state. This weighed heavily on Uncle Ed, who rented an apartment in Portland so he could spend alternate weekends making sure James didn't succumb to his congenital wanderlust, or step on any other bear traps. With Ed's steady presence, James satisfied the conditions of his parole, then immediately took to the open road on another Harley. By the time this drama was over and Ed returned home,

Nadine had just opened her drapery store in Twin Peaks. It was an immediate, if modest, success, and Ed felt obliged to be supportive as Nadine worked around the clock, which tossed yet another railroad tie on the tracks in front of Ed finally getting together with Norma. Stalemate. Hurley Luck.

A decade passed, as they do. James eventually came back to Twin Peaks, in 2006—this time on a Trailways bus. He'd totaled his Harley in an accident involving a runaway coal truck in West Virginia some months before. Hurley Luck being what it apparently is, he suffered a compound fracture of his leg and ended up flat broke in a county rehab facility. James had edged past thirty, and at this point the bloom faded permanently from his Kerouac romance with the road. Once his leg healed up, he went back to work for Ed at the Gas Farm, and a few years later he took a second job working night security at the Great Northern. He lives alone, modestly, drives a used Ford Focus now, still plays guitar, writes plaintive, simple, and appealing songs—unrequited love, heartbreak, and so on—that he sometimes performs locally, and as far as I can tell has never hurt another human being.

As I pieced together how James Hurley's life unfolded, this truth they taught at Quantico came back to me, Chief: Just as any criminal can be an accessory to a crime, an entirely innocent person close to an act of violence can become a collateral victim. You can call it Hurley Luck, but this could have happened to anybody; it just seems to me that a part of James died when Laura did, and it has haunted him ever since.

You'll be pleased to learn that happier outcomes lay in store for a few others in town whom I know you're fond of. As she soldiered through her troubled private life, Norma Jennings threw all her available energies during these years into the Double R, making it a center of community pride during hard times. When the lumber industry in the valley died and the Packard Mill was shuttered, a lot of people were out of work. She extended credit and reduced prices to families she knew were hurting and made all her excess food available to the homeless. When the economy recovered, Norma took a leap of faith into franchising her beloved eatery—she even briefly dated the big-city slicker from a "comfort food" corporation who wanted to make "Norma's" a household name in a number of other locations throughout the Pacific Northwest.

This decades-old logjam began to break up late one night when Nadine was doing her books in the back office of Run Silent, Run Drapes. While surfing the Net, she stumbled across an episode of Dr. Amp's nightly rant. Recognizing her former therapist immediately, she was hooked like a trout. With the unique kind of fervor she could bring to lunatic causes, Nadine soon bought herself a mail-order golden shovel, and a few more for people on her Christmas list. She installed one of the golden shovels like a holy relic in the display window of her drapery store, while embracing the entire Dr. Amp lifestyle: drinking the "Dr. Amp" hemp protein shakes, doing the "Dr. Amp 'Walking in Nature Program,'" following his rigorous "Crusade for Political Renewal" by donating to a variety of nonprofit charities he supports. (Taken in its totality, Dr. Amp's brand, if you will, is one part Amway, one part Anthony Robbins by way of Timothy Leary, one part Grateful Dead.) Nadine's enthusiasm quickly turned into a kind of religious devotion that appeared to do for her what thirty-odd years of traditional and crackpot therapeutic approaches had failed to achieve: It restored her to a balanced, happy, and functional life.

During one of his weekly nocturnal supply runs, Dr. Jacoby noticed one of his spotlit golden shovels hanging in Nadine's window. He stopped, knocked on the door, and laid eyes on his former client for the first time in more than two decades. I can't tell you exactly what they talked about—although rumors suggest they may now be dating—but less than two weeks later, Nadine marched over to the Gas Farm and forthrightly handed Ed his walking papers, the release from obligatory matrimonial bonds he'd long ago given up hoping he would ever receive.

That same day, Big Ed Hurley, pushing seventy, in front of the lunch rush at the Double R Diner, proposed to Norma Jennings, who, it turned out, was just at that moment giving the city slicker and his plans to take "Norma's" diner corporate the heave-ho. To paraphrase Vince Lombardi, timing isn't everything, it's the only thing.

You'll be pleased to learn, I think, that Ed and Norma got married not long after. James played a song he wrote on his guitar during a civil ceremony conducted by the Big Log near the old train station. All of their friends—half the town, it seems—were there. Andy Brennan bawled more or less throughout, and I'm told even Deputy Chief Hawk got a tear in his eye. His old friend Big Ed's Hurley Luck had finally turned.

INITIAL *TP* DATE 9/6/17

# FEDERAL BUREAU OF INVESTIGATION

CASE #  008-072-0119  BUREAU FILE #  TP-12/18

# MARGARET COULSON

PRESTON, Tamara

CASE AGENT  *TP*

INITIAL

# CONFIDENTIAL

FIELD OFFICE CRIMINAL INVESTIGATIVE
AND ADMINISTRATIVE FILES

See also Nos.  001-43-25

222-87

FEDERAL BUREAU
OF INVESTIGATION

*Field Office Criminal Investigative
and Administrative Files*

As you know, just prior to your arrival back in Twin Peaks, Margaret Coulson—known locally as the Log Lady—passed away after a long battle with lung cancer. In the weeks and days before her death, we learned that she made a significant contribution to the Cooper investigation, one that led to a breakthrough from the Twin Peaks Sheriff's Department's side of the case. Her funeral was widely attended—the newspaper said it seemed that the entire town had turned out—on the shores of Pearl Lake. There was no conventional service, but people were invited to speak if they wished to pay tribute, and many, many people got up to share their favorite Log Lady stories.

Deputy Hawk was the last to speak, and he read from a page that he said Margaret had given him the day before she passed. He sent this on to me, and I include the text here:

> *Every meeting between friends must end with a parting, and*
> *so, my friends, today we take our leave. This is life. None of us*
> *profits from ignoring or hiding from the facts, so why should we*
> *bother? Life is what it is, a gift that is given to us for a time—like*
> *a library book—that must eventually be returned. How should*
> *we treat this book? If we are able to remember that it is not*
> *ours to begin with—one that we're entrusted with, to care for,*
> *to study and learn from—perhaps it would change the way we*
> *treat it while it's in our possession. How do you treat a precious*
> *gift from a dear friend? This is a good question to ask, and*
> *today is a good time to ask it.*
>
> *Such busy, busy minds we have. Have you noticed? We*
> *think and we think until we twist ourselves into the ground like*
> *a flathead screw. My log has this to say: The answers to all our*
> *questions are in the wind and the trees, the rocks and the water.*

*No one is helpless. No one is beyond helping. It is good to seek out those who need us and do what we can for them. I recommend that. There is nothing that can't be done if we set our minds to doing it. Don't be sad. Be happy you have another day to do what needs doing. We only have so many of them.*

*We are born into this world, not another one. It's not perfect, but it is what it is. This world presents some simple, certain truths. It helps us grow if we accept them, but many of these truths seem to trouble or frighten us. For instance, there is no light without darkness—and this troubles many of us— but without it, how else would we tell one from the other? We spend half of every day in darkness; surely we should make our peace with this. You may decide to see this as a metaphor. Many people do. I see it as a fact. Metaphors are beautiful ways of speaking about the truth. So are facts. Both tell us that time— and light, and darkness—moves in cycles. We move through them, too, often as passengers, but if our eyes are open, there is much to be learned along the way. A traveler learns more than a passenger. When darkness comes, a traveler learns to be brave, for they know the light will return. Anyone who's spent a night alone in the woods learns this.*

*When a dark age comes, hold the light inside. That's where it lives anyway. There are forces of darkness—and beings of darkness—and they are real and have always been around us. They're part of the dance, just as you and I are; they're just listening to different music. This may be the most troubling truth we will ever know. Many of us live most of our lives and brush up against this reality only rarely. It is far from pleasant, but wishing it were otherwise will not make it so.*

*So may I offer a suggestion: When a dark age comes, just as you would at night, hold the light inside you. Others, I can tell you, have already learned to do the same. In time, you will learn to recognize the light, in yourself and others. In this way you will find each other. Together, you will make the light stronger.*

*This truth I know as sure as the dawn: Darkness will always yield to light, when the light is strong.*

Margaret asked that her ashes be scattered in the Ghostwood Forest, and so they were later that day by members of the Sheriff's Department. She left her log to Hawk. He keeps it on his mantel. He reports that it hasn't said anything to him yet, but he says he's "keeping an ear open, just in case."

With all I've learned about Twin Peaks, Chief, and all you've told me, my only regret is that I never got to meet Margaret. As you know, I don't consider myself a religious person, but when I read these words of hers, sometimes I think maybe I'll get my chance someday. (To meet her; not to become religious.)

INITIAL *TP*   DATE 9, 6, 17

# FEDERAL BUREAU OF INVESTIGATION

CASE #     008-072-0119          BUREAU FILE #     TP-13/18

# SHERIFF HARRY
# TRUMAN

PRESTON, Tamara

**CASE AGENT**          *TP*

INITIAL

# CONFIDENTIAL

FIELD OFFICE CRIMINAL INVESTIGATIVE
AND ADMINISTRATIVE FILES

See also Nos.   26-67-701
001-43-25
3312

FEDERAL BUREAU
OF INVESTIGATION

*Field Office Criminal Investigative
and Administrative Files*

You specifically asked me to find out why Sheriff Harry Truman had left his post, as you discovered upon your return to Twin Peaks. Agent Cooper's fondness for his friend and former colleague is well established, and the reasons are abundantly clear. Truman was everything a local law enforcement officer should be: sensitive to the needs of his community, protecting and serving in equal measure, modest in word and deed, and as solid and dependable as the sunrise.

In the aftermath of the Palmer case, however, Truman was nearly finished by a defining trauma of his own: his ruinous relationship with the dangerous sociopath Josie Packard. I believe the staunch support Agent Cooper offered his friend after her death helped preserve his sanity, and may well have saved him from self-violence. The sheriff had clearly been damaged by his loss, but not irreparably so: Harry Truman was made of sterner stuff. He'd lived his whole life in Twin Peaks, son of the town's previous sheriff, as you know. I've studied his entire career. While Harry could at many times have smudged the line between extracurricular vigilantism and the strict limits of the law—specifically through the offices of the local "social club" he eventually led, known as the Bookhouse Boys—a closer examination of their history has convinced me that the Boys have always acted in accordance with the spirit of the patriotic home guard Truman's father founded during World War II. In my opinion, the Bookhouse Boys represent a moral counterweight to the many recent and negative examples we've seen of homegrown rural—and so-called libertarian—militias.

As badly hurt as he was by Josie's betrayal, I believe Harry may have been even more haunted by the sudden disappearance of his friend Cooper. From the records I've come across in his files, Harry never abandoned his own investigation into what happened to Cooper—some of those details, pertinent to our own work, are included later in this document—and that for the next twenty-plus years he never gave up on it.

Harry reached retirement age recently, and as you know, the story told around town—that he had turned in his badge for a fishing pole and a seat on the sidelines—was not true. I've confirmed that, just as his brother Frank told you on the phone, six months before your return there, Harry had learned he was seriously ill. (I've confirmed that it's cancer, and he's still living and undergoing treatment in a research hospital near Seattle, but he's fighting uphill.) Typically private, unwilling to burden anyone with his troubles, Harry kept this news from everyone at the station and in town. His older brother, Frank—who had recently retired after his own long and distinguished career in law enforcement in western Washington—seems to have been the only one he told about his illness, although Hawk, who knew Harry better than anyone, figured it out right away. Frank agreed to move back to Twin Peaks and take the job for two years to help stabilize the department, with the understanding that he would then step down and hand the reins to Hawk.

My sense of this, Chief, is that, given his personal regard for you, if you made the effort to reach out to Harry, he would respond, and be more than grateful to hear from you.

INITIAL *TP*  DATE 9, 6, 17

# FEDERAL BUREAU OF INVESTIGATION

CASE #    **008-072-0119**      BUREAU FILE #    **TP-14/18**

# MAJOR BRIGGS

PRESTON, Tamara

**CASE AGENT**

INITIAL *TP*

# CONFIDENTIAL

FIELD OFFICE CRIMINAL INVESTIGATIVE
AND ADMINISTRATIVE FILES

See also Nos.   69-02-0024

001-43-25

8813

009-60-23

FEDERAL BUREAU
OF INVESTIGATION

*Field Office Criminal Investigative
and Administrative Files*

So much of what brought us back to Twin Peaks—and ultimately led to our finding Agent Cooper—we clearly owe to Major Garland Briggs. The dossier he compiled and left for us, with its multitude of intriguing leads and frankly incredible tales, is a puzzle we'll still be reviewing and unraveling for years to come. Among the questions we haven't settled—even in the aftermath of resolving Cooper's disappearance—is what exactly happened to Major Briggs himself. Here's what we know and what I've put together about the time line:

We know that the man whom Sheriff Truman found in the sycamore grove after Agent Cooper's disappearance was not, in fact, Agent Cooper, but his Double.

We know that when Cooper's Double checked himself out of the hospital the next day, it paid Briggs a visit at his home. We know that Briggs had been expecting a visit from his new Blue Rose "control," after the death of Doug Milford, and he may have assumed, or even been told, that Agent Cooper was going to be that control. During the Double's visit, Briggs became alarmed by their interaction and wrote about it in his final entry of the dossier. Given his intuitive capacities, it's not too great a supposition to assume that Briggs realized, at some point during their meeting, that the man in front of him was *not* Agent Cooper—and that this was the reason for the Mayday call that he wrote as the last words in the dossier. We can also assume Major Briggs realized that, rather than confront the Double, he'd best keep that realization to himself, but, given what we have since learned about the Double, it's fair to suppose that it saw through Briggs's intention.

We know from Mrs. Briggs that, shortly after the Double left their house, Briggs departed for Listening Post Alpha, his classified Blue Rose station up in the mountains. "Mayday protocols" required him to secure—or destroy—all of the secure data contained there, and also stipulated that he disable—or destroy—most of the more advanced and classified technology he'd been using to conduct his study. When Briggs got there, one of two things then happened: Either he successfully enacted those measures and then staged a scene to make it look as if the post had been ransacked—and that he himself had been attacked—or, at some time during his staging, the Double arrived and a genuine and deadly sacking and assault took place.

In either case, given the DNA evidence found at the scene—Briggs's fingerprints, blood, and tissue—the forensic impressions seemed clear: The post had been breached, during which Briggs had, in all likelihood, been attacked. A few days later, when the wreckage of Briggs's car was found at the bottom of a nearby canyon—with a charred, unidentifiable corpse inside and a few of Briggs's teeth conveniently placed nearby—death by accident became, as you know, the official conclusion of the investigation. (Reports of the attack were suppressed by our internal investigators, and no suspects were ever publicly identified). It's clear now that the only reasonable suspect was the Double, and I believe it's likely he followed Briggs up the mountain to the LPA later that same day. Briggs appears to have conducted such an elaborate deception to fool exactly one person: the Double. That effort appears, at least at the time, to have succeeded.

Given what we have subsequently learned, I believe it's reasonable to conclude that the scene at the LPA was—for the most part—staged by Briggs and that he subsequently escaped with whatever classified material he could carry with him, which I believe later became the basis for the dossier. A few miles from the outpost, Briggs then staged the crash of his own vehicle, leaving a severely burned corpse inside to complete the illusion and facilitate his escape. If and when the Double arrived at the scene after Briggs had already left, he most likely made his own search of the property, departed with whatever he found, and perhaps set the fire to cover his tracks. I believe it's less likely, but still possible, that the Double arrived while Briggs was still on-site, but there were sufficient security measures in place that Briggs had ample warning of his approach, giving him enough time to escape before the Double actually got there. (This all remains impossible to determine with 100 percent accuracy.) What, if any, data the Double itself took away from the LPA, we can't actually know, but if his arrival rushed Briggs's departure in any way, it's possible that the Major may have left something pertinent behind.

Both Briggs and the Double then vanished from sight for the next twenty-five years. Here's where the story gets dicey, and by that I mean "the laws of time and space as we understand them may not necessarily apply." (As you know, the following is based primarily on testimony gathered from our main eyewitness in Buckhorn, South Dakota, the now deceased high school principal, William Hastings, whom I questioned personally.)

For the past few years, Hastings and his girlfriend—local librarian Ruth Davenport—had been dabbling in speculative esoteric/occult research. Together they authored an amateur blog about their work, which they posted on the Internet. They titled it *The Search for the Zone*. According to Hastings's testimony, at some point during their last year together, they claimed to have made contact with a person or entity that identified itself only as "The Major." They were eventually told they could make personal contact with this individual by entering into some sort of nonphysical or metaphysical dimension. The Major told them that this encounter would occur at a specific time and place in or near an unspecified entrance to this "Zone." The location he gave them for the meeting happened to be a derelict vacant lot on the wrong side of the tracks in Buckhorn.

Once they were "inside" the Zone, "the Major"—whom Hastings described as "hiding" or "hibernating" inside of wherever this was—appeared and tasked them with finding a set of "important coordinates" from a secure military database. (From Hastings's description, it seems that during this initial conversation, "the Major" revealed himself to them in more or less corporeal physical form.) As we've now been able to confirm, once Hastings and Davenport succeeded in hacking this military database—most likely with clues provided by the Major—and obtained the information he was after, they returned to the same location of the "Zone" a *second* time to personally deliver it to "the Major." As they were about to give the Major these coordinates, according to Bill Hastings, all manner of hell broke loose. The Major floated up—toward what he described as a vortex or "portal," presumably like the one you yourself witnessed, Chief—and dark, shadowy figures, appearing out of nowhere, assaulted them. Both Davenport and "the Major" were decapitated in the attack, and Hastings was left unconscious, but alive, in the vacant lot. He seemed to suffer some form of memory loss about this event, and his memory returned only after his arrest.

A few days later, Davenport's severed head, aligned perversely and tenderly on the neck of the body of "The Major," was discovered by local police in her apartment. This eventually led to our involvement and our arrival in Buckhorn, including our interrogation of Hastings. It also led, weeks later, to our discovery of Briggs's secret dossier—which one has to assume Briggs also gave to Hastings and Davenport at their first meeting, and which Davenport had concealed in a basement storage locker in her apartment building. This suggests, to my mind, that wherever he'd "been" for the past quarter of a century, the Major had taken the dossier with him.

The body was identified as that of Major Garland Briggs, and his age was determined to be roughly forty-five, which just happened to be how old he was at the time of his disappearance, twenty-five years ago. Shortly after Buckhorn police took Hastings into custody, his wife, Phyllis, was shot to death—allegedly by her attorney/lover, who shortly thereafter also died when his car exploded. This entire local crime wave, the preponderance of evidence now confirms, was committed by the Double and his henchmen.

To recap: Hastings attempted to show us the site of this entrance to the Zone, where we discovered the body of Ruth Davenport in a vacant lot—and where you had your own glimpse of the Zone—during which time Hastings was mysteriously killed, assaulted by an unseen assailant more or less right in front of our eyes. The coordinates the two of them had given to the Major were found on the arm of Ruth Davenport, where she'd apparently written them down in order to verbally relay them to the Major; Hastings indicated that he'd cautioned them to put nothing on paper. Those coordinates eventually led us back to Twin Peaks, the truth about "Diane," and the final collision at the sheriff's station between Cooper and the Double.

Do we doubt that any of this actually happened? It's hard to argue with when, for a large part of all that ensued, *we* were eyewitnesses.

So: Where exactly had Major Briggs been "hiding" or "hibernating" for twenty-five years? After faking his own death, did he make the ultimate escape? Did he slip inside some sort of "portal" near Twin Peaks—its location revealed by these aforementioned coordinates—where time proceeded to stand still for twenty-five years while he evaded the Double? Given our Bureau training—or dare I say *bias*?—to regard our human existence as a "science-based reality," how is this idea something we can even consider as remotely possible? And yet we have before us a substantial amount of what one is compelled to concede is supporting evidence—exhibit A, the forty-five-year-old body of Major Briggs—which appears impossible to refute. For the purposes of my report, let's accept that as a "known unknown." But we can take it further: the idea of these "coordinates" revealing—okay, I'll say it—the existence of *multiple* locations of entrances into what I'll label (for our internal discussion only) "other space-time dimensions" is the next conundrum confronting us. Certainly, "the Major" making entrances in Twin Peaks and an exit in Buckhorn to meet with Hastings and Davenport suggests that at least one other such "portal" exists. Once again, you have your own eyewitness experience in Buckhorn to draw on here, Chief: In your own words, that portal seemed to lead *somewhere.*

It also implies this: Since it's clear that Hastings and Davenport "hacked" this information on the Major's behalf from what they told us was one of our governmental agencies, it suggests that we already had this information in our possession. And Briggs *knew* it was there. Does this imply the same thing to you that it does to me? That—I'm speculating—Major Briggs knew about all this because, near the end of his own life, Doug Milford gave it to him. That Milford or Briggs—or both of them—figured out that Listening Post Alpha had *gathered* such beyond-classified information, which, I've come to understand, is more or less our stated mission. More than possible. But is it also possible that the Major *didn't* initially realize all that they had? Did something in the conversation Briggs conducted with the Double at his house that day tip the Major off to this information's existence, or, at the least, to a relevance he hadn't previously realized it held?

My question to you is: Was it us? Did the Blue Rose Task Force possess this information? Was it actually *our* servers that Hastings and Davenport hacked into? A high school principal and a librarian? For crying out loud, who were these people, Russian sleeper agents? (That was a joke, Chief, but the idea that these amateurs penetrated our servers is not.) Not willing to give them that much credit, I'll offer another scenario: Briggs knew about the Blue Rose Task Force, so is it possible that—near the end, when he realized the Double was coming for him—he stashed the information inside some innocuous digital cutout where he knew no one else would look for it? We've since learned from Twin Peaks law enforcement that the Major hid a similar clue, to the local set of coordinates, for his son, Bobby, in plain sight—concealed in his favorite armchair. I believe this argues for the second option as the more likely: Briggs stashed the information in a place that would not have posed insurmountable entry barriers to amateurs like these two Buckhorn rubes, in a place where no professional would even think to look for it. Misdirection. (I'm rooting for this interpretation, by the way, for obvious reasons.)

Now let's ask ourselves what the Double was up to in all of this, from his opening move.

We know that Agent Cooper "disappeared" somewhere in the Ghostwood Forest that night more than twenty-five years ago, in pursuit of Windom Earle. We know that he reappeared the next morning, along with Annie Blackburn, and was found by Sheriff Truman. We can also say, with a high degree of certainty, that this particular "he" was the Double; this was its first confirmed appearance. Which means that the real Cooper was—most likely—still "inside" wherever he'd disappeared into the night before. There are indications in many of the accounts I've examined—on and between the lines—that Cooper had found his way into some kind of out-of-time place or portal similar to the Zone described by Major Briggs. (For instance: The ancient pictographs on the walls of Owl Cave are alleged to depict how access to such a place is attained.) Deputy Hawk is on the record citing a local Native American legend to describe this particular place. His people called it the Black Lodge. I'm going to suggest, for the sake of convenience, that we call it this, too. (Or if that term doesn't work for you, I suggest we refer to it as something like "the Hotel California," in that "you can check in, but you can never leave," at least not for twenty-five years.)

Once the Double disappeared from Twin Peaks after his meeting with Briggs, he utterly vanished. Every maximum-alert all-points bulletin issued around the world by the Bureau failed to turn up any trace of him for the next quarter century, save two. There was a surveillance photo of the Double from a South American sting operation, which certainly appears to be him, though analysis did reveal hints of digital manipulation, so in the Photoshop era, it may be impossible to authenticate. The second: Cooper appears, more clearly, on another surveillance photo from the bizarre "glass box" operation/murder scene that you and Albert investigated more recently in Manhattan. Connecting these distant dots yielded the following conclusion, which, thanks to a boatload of forensic digging and dedicated effort across a multitude of disciplines during the past year, I have now been able to substantiate:

Based on these findings, during his twenty-five years on the loose, the Double appears to have established and run an international criminal syndicate to rival any cartel or crime family in recent memory. This organization appears to have inserted its tendrils into nearly every known vehicle for vice in the lexicon: gambling, drugs, cybercrime, human trafficking, prostitution, murder for hire, illegal banking, stock manipulation, extortion, blackmail, insurance fraud. (About the only criminal arena missing from the list is politics—aside from a few obvious bribes made to elected foreign officials—but chances are that'll turn up eventually.)

All the proceeds from this baroque, elaborate spiderweb—minus expenses and payoffs, of course—funneled directly to the top, to *him,* through a dense and complicated network of shell companies, LLCs, offshore banking, and the complicit, well-compensated participation of a number of known corrupt regimes and broken states. The entirety of the operation will take many years to unravel, but our early and likely overly conservative estimates suggest that the net payoff to the man at the top was in the billions.

Although the Double appeared to somehow travel freely throughout the world—establishing residences and businesses in a dozen different places, among them Las Vegas, Berlin, Amsterdam, Buenos Aires, the island of Cyprus, and Istanbul—he doesn't appear to have amassed all of these resources for the usual, more or less banal criminal outlets or indulgences we're accustomed to seeing: greed, lust, materialism, self-interested power, etc. Instead he appears to have been employing this growing fortune for what I would suggest we call "research." The Double was after something. Hunting something, and maybe more than just one thing. Here's what we know:

He desperately wanted those coordinates from Briggs. He pursued him across a quarter century, even after an official public finding that the Major had died in that car crash, and he never relented. If Briggs ever came out of hiding—from whatever manner of "space" he was hiding in—prior to appearing in Buckhorn, we have no record of it. But it's clear that the second time the Major emerged to meet Hastings and Davenport, the Double was there waiting for him. He killed Briggs, Davenport, Hastings, and anyone else who got in the way, seized those coordinates, and headed for their location, more or less directly, by way of the South Dakota prison and our former confidential FBI/Blue Rose informant, Ray Monroe.

(Absent any information from Monroe—also subsequently murdered by the Double—it seems clear that the Double went to all the trouble of breaking *into* prison and breaking *out* with Monroe because the latter had some kind of information the Double wanted. I'll circle back to this shortly.)

The "glass box" operation in New York, which we now know the Double set up through a series of cutouts, suggests he was after something else as well. Some kind of entity that moved, as Briggs appeared to be able to do, free of the constraints of time and space as we used to think we understood them. Something monstrous and murderous that appeared in that box and slaughtered those two kids who had the horrible misfortune of being there when it appeared. From the evidence we've seen, the only familiar word that comes to mind to properly describe this entity is "demonic." And the glass box appears to have been installed there as a trap to catch it.

Let's examine its motives in the first instance: The Double seems to have wanted these coordinates to gain entrance to whatever space they led to, to find the "place" where Briggs had been hiding, a location or dimension where time appeared to stand still. (This sounds crazy even as I'm writing it, but we've both seen things during the course of this investigation, Chief, that are even "crazier" than this, so I'll just run with it.) Was this "portal" the only one of its kind? Or was it just one of many entrances, like a subway stop into some sort of mysterious network or web that could be accessed from many different places? That seems likely. My thought is this: What if the Double was looking for the most *important* location in this alleged system, a Grand Central Station, if you will, on the other side?

Final question, and it's one that all the others lead to: What did the Double want, if it ever actually made it to this place? What was it after? Some kind or form of even greater power than it already appeared to possess? (What would that be? Immortality?) I mean, I don't think it was trying to get there just to lodge a complaint or plead a case with whoever was in charge, do you?

I want to take a step back for a moment: Let's consider the very *existence* of the Double. You'll recall the mythological location I mentioned earlier— the Black Lodge, a hellish place of origin for people, entities, or creatures walking the "dark path," posthumously referenced by Margaret Coulson in her funeral remarks. Deputy Chief Hawk also once spoke of another spiritual concept that may be related, called the Dweller on the Threshold. (Agent Cooper mentioned hearing about it from Hawk in one of his tapes to Diane.) This "Dweller" is said to represent the sum total of all the dark, negative, unresolved qualities that reside in every human being. (There are also esoteric theories that the same idea can apply to the fate of nations, but let's confine this to the more personal concept for now.)

The Dweller legend states that when a person on the spiritual path consciously approaches a place or state of soulful enlightenment, at the very moment they're about to enter into its full embrace—on the "threshold," as it were—this Dweller allegedly appears and must be confronted and defeated in order for the person to successfully pass through. As with most mythology, my presumption had been that this figure is allegorical, a metaphor for a struggle that takes place in the realm of the intrapersonal and psychological. Not a *literal* concept.

But now I have to ask: Is this, literally, what Cooper's Double was? Albert and I have spoken of this thing before as a "*tulpa.*" A *tulpa*—like the false "Diane"—is a concept that in the original Tibetan, it turns out, does not mean "double" or "doppelganger" but rather an entity created or summoned by a dark magician or sorcerer, through the practice of ancient and corrupt forms of esoteric magic: necromancy, demons, devil worship. Madame Helena Petrovna Blavatsky, who wrote extensively about these matters in the nineteenth century—setting aside for a moment the many arguments about whether or not she was an outright charlatan—referred to this sect as "the Brothers of the Shadow." I bring this up to make the point that the Dweller scenario, in the Double's case, at least, seems more likely to me than the *tulpa.*

If we continue along these lines, is there a *third* alternative theory worth considering—simpler, perhaps, but no less fantastic? This is directly related to another controversial concept you told me about from the original Laura Palmer case: While in custody, shortly before his death, Leland Palmer claimed to be possessed by a demonic entity called BOB, and he attributed his actions to its lifelong, malign influence over him. I've gone over all the evidence and contemporary accounts. They are bone-chilling, to the point where—had Leland survived—one wonders if an exorcism might have been more efficacious than a criminal trial.

Which leads me to pose *this* possibility: Was the Double somehow similarly possessed? I realize we can't settle this debate with absolute certainty, or even a fraction of it, but I also think it's worth asking whether all these concepts fit together—logic and method be damned—and point toward something that's so far out of our perception that we'll never begin to grasp it if we don't tremendously enlarge our frame of reference.

We saw what happened at the sheriff's station. There were close to twenty witnesses, including you, me, and Albert. We agree that we saw more or less the same thing: At the moment of its death, something appeared to rise up out of the Double and disappear: something *not* Cooper.

And we know that no sooner had Cooper appeared to "defeat" this . . . whatever it was . . . than he almost immediately appeared at the location of the coordinates that his damn double was after from the start—and you went with him, Chief—and from there Cooper promptly disappeared *again* and hasn't been seen since. And Cooper's former assistant, the *real* Diane— who had just appeared out of *nowhere* in a downstairs holding cell not long before all this happened—disappeared right along with him.

(Do I need to revisit the false—or *tulpa*—"Diane" that we all saw die in a Buckhorn motel room a few days earlier when she pulled a gun on the three of us? I mean, honestly, are they cranking out these duplicate creatures in an alternate-reality Kinko's with some kind of Lovecraftian 3-D printer? Pardon my French for a second, Chief, but what the fuck?)

You've described to me what happened when you left with Cooper: The lights went out in the sheriff's station. (I was there for that part.) You somehow found yourself in the basement of the Great Northern Hotel with Cooper. Something then "opened up" in a boiler room in the basement of the Great Northern, which you described as an "endless corridor." You exchanged parting words. Cooper entered into it. This corridor, shortly thereafter, closed. Cooper was gone. You were back in what appeared to be, as far as you could determine by any other measure, an ordinary boiler room.

\* \* \*

Okay.

There's one last outlier in this fractured fairy tale that I feel the need to bring up now. References to him pop up far more than coincidence can account for, around the margins of this whole narrative. I'm speaking, centrally, of a man I never knew, a celebrated Bureau veteran, your former classmate and colleague, the man you called the "guiding inspiration" of the Blue Rose Task Force.

INITIAL *TP* DATE 9 , 6 , 17

**FEDERAL BUREAU OF INVESTIGATION**

CASE #    008-072-0119      BUREAU FILE #    TP-15/18

# PHILLIP JEFFRIES

_____

_____

_____

PRESTON, Tamara

_____
CASE AGENT

_____
INITIAL _TP_

# CONFIDENTIAL

| FIELD OFFICE CRIMINAL INVESTIGATIVE |
| AND ADMINISTRATIVE FILES |

See also Nos. 001-43-25        _____

     93-0811               _____

       002                  _____

_____        _____

_____        _____

In Cooper's files, he mentions a strange scene that supposedly took place in our Philadelphia offices in 1989. (I have not found any corroboration of this in other Bureau records, by the way: Did you have them erased?) Phillip Jeffries had been on an extended and highly classified Blue Rose assignment that involved a long-term posting in Buenos Aires, Argentina. At some point during that assignment, while working undercover, Jeffries disappeared—every bit as abruptly as Cooper disappeared from Twin Peaks twenty-five years ago, without a trace.

The difference being: On February 16, after spending six months completely off the Bureau's radar, Phillip Jeffries showed up, without warning, in our offices in Philadelphia. He was wearing a white linen suit more appropriate for a tropical clime—it was the middle of a particularly nasty winter in Philadelphia, but summer in Argentina. Cooper described Jeffries as "distraught and disoriented." When he asked and was told what date and year it was, Jeffries seemed generally horrified, and reacted with outright panic. He also seemed confused and troubled by Cooper's being there and seemed to believe he wasn't who he appeared to be. (Cooper indicated in his notes that this conversation took place in your office, Chief, and that you and Albert were also present.) Moments later, right in the middle of the conversation, apparently the three of you looked over and realized that Jeffries was gone. Vanished. And, as near as I can tell, the man was never seen or heard from again. Not in Philadelphia nor Buenos Aires—where Jeffries had, by the way, been seen by multiple witnesses in the lobby of his hotel *that same morning, at roughly the same time, while wearing the same damn tropical outfit*—or anywhere else on God's green earth.

Two questions, Chief: How did Phillip Jeffries manage to be, or so it seems, in two places thousands of miles and a continent apart on the same day at the same time? Why was he so distraught upon learning what *year* it was? Why would he ask a question like that in the first place?

Let's break this down. I've read every word I could find about Jeffries. He was, according to every account, a brilliant man, the only son of an old aristocratic Virginia family and a phenomenally talented law enforcement officer. One comment about him in all his profiles stood out for me: "This world wasn't enough for him." You yourself wrote that. You knew the man better than anyone else, and you and he founded the Blue Rose Task Force together. You've confirmed to me that Jeffries was deeply and openly interested in a variety of esoteric and occult subjects, including things that one could have ripped from the ripest pages of pulp science fiction.

I know the Blue Rose Task Force is charged with the investigation of matters that would make most average citizens—or the world's most expert neurophysicists, for that matter—flee from the room with their hair spontaneously combusting. I know now that during its decades of operation, long before I came on the scene, you and Jeffries encountered phenomena that both of you struggled to understand or describe. What I went looking for was the moment when Phillip Jeffries stopped investigating these things and started living them.

The conclusion I would submit is this: It happened in Buenos Aires. I've tracked down the few scraps of information he left behind there, and one item in particular stands out. Although he went to Argentina in 1986 to investigate what appeared to be an international criminal enterprise, he very quickly focused in on an aspect of the case that I believe we've misunderstood all these years. Within his first month, Jeffries identified a shadowy suspect, someone he believed could be the central person of interest in charge of this entire operation. All he had, at first, was a name he mentioned that same day in your office:

# FEDERAL BUREAU OF INVESTIGATION

CASE #   008-072-0119          BUREAU FILE #   TP-16/18

## JUDY

PRESTON, Tamara

CASE AGENT                    *TP*

INITIAL

# CONFIDENTIAL

FIELD OFFICE CRIMINAL INVESTIGATIVE
AND ADMINISTRATIVE FILES

See also Nos. 001-43-25
744-5
8818

FEDERAL BUREAU
OF INVESTIGATION

*Field Office Criminal Investigative
and Administrative Files*

I know this because Cooper is also on record, on one of his tapes to Diane from this period, about the only part of this conversation that took place in your office that he could *exactly* recall. Apparently the first words out of Jeffries's mouth were these: "I'm not going to talk about Judy; in fact, we're not going to talk about Judy at all, we're going to keep her out of it." (Can you also confirm this for me, Chief?)

Someone named Judy. At least, that's who Cooper and everyone else in the task force assumed he was talking about. Until I discovered something recently, carved into the wall of his former Buenos Aires hotel room, near the phone, beneath a layer of new wallpaper that was added in 1997. It appeared to be the same name, but the spelling was different:

Joudy.

Carved, not written, deeply and hurriedly, with what appears to have been a pocketknife. Next to the phone. As if he'd heard something on a call and had to carve it right there on the wall. Not with a pen or a pencil, but a knife. Why would someone do that? Because this information upset him? Because it affected him to such a degree that only a weapon could express the depth and intensity of whatever he was feeling at the time?

Joudy. So who was this person, and why would just a *name* have that kind of impact on Phillip Jeffries? We know that, previously, he'd thought the name of the shadowy figure he was pursuing was Judy. Now he apparently had new information. An extra vowel. A slightly altered pronunciation. But what else did this change—what more did this tell him?

I've done some research of my own.

Joudy, it turns out, is also the name of an ancient entity in Sumerian mythology. (This dates back to at least 3000 B.C.) The name was used to describe a species of wandering demon—also generically known as an *utukku*—that had "escaped from the underworld" and roamed freely throughout the earth, where they feasted on human flesh and, allegedly, ripped the souls from their victims, which provided even more meaningful nourishment. They particularly thrived while feeding—and I quote—"on human suffering." These beings were said to appear in both male and female forms—"Joudy" indicated the female, and the male was known as "Ba'al"—and, while they were considered beyond dangerous individually, if a male and a female ever *united* while on the earth, the ancient texts claimed, their resulting "marriage" would create something far more peril-ous. As in: the end of the world as we know it. A few centuries later, Ba'al becomes better known, in both Christian and Islamic sources, as "Beelzebub," a false god, or, as he's known more generally and generically today, the devil.

Do I have your attention yet, Chief?

So what do we do with this information? How does it change the focus of what we're looking at here, if at all? What concrete leads was Jeffries on to? Are these just the insane ramblings of a man who, as you well know, swam in a sea filled with extravagant and esoteric conspiracy theories, a sure sign that he'd lost not only his way but his mind? Or do we calmly sit with this information and see whether, and how, it fits into what we already know? In other words: Do our jobs.

INITIAL _TP_   DATE 9/6/17

# FEDERAL BUREAU OF INVESTIGATION

CASE #    008-072-0119          BUREAU FILE #    TP-17/18

## RAY MONROE

PRESTON, Tamara

CASE AGENT

INITIAL *TP*

# CONFIDENTIAL

FIELD OFFICE CRIMINAL INVESTIGATIVE
AND ADMINISTRATIVE FILES

See also Nos.

9 4 4 – 5

08 7312

*Field Office Criminal Investigative
and Administrative Files*

There's one additional piece here that's crucial to consider before we proceed. Ray Monroe, the deep-cover informant who apparently was recruited by someone involved with our task force to work on the "missing Cooper" case, succeeded in making contact with "the Double." Strong evidence suggests that Monroe penetrated his inner circle, met with him, and worked with him in the weeks or months prior to the Double's surfacing in Buckhorn, South Dakota. I've come across a vague reference that indicates that Monroe, two years before Buckhorn, began working this operation in Las Vegas, where we know the Double had established part of his empire, with Duncan Todd as his local principal operative. I believe this is where Monroe's first contact with the target may have taken place.

In a partially garbled phone message to an agency cutout, Monroe claimed he was reporting directly to someone inside the Blue Rose Task Force, but he never specified who it was. (If it was you, Chief, I believe you would have told us, wouldn't you?) After the Double succeeded in breaking into and out of that South Dakota prison—taking Monroe with him—we know that at some point before he died, Monroe made a phone call on a burner found at the location in Montana where we also found Monroe's body. Based on data retrieved from that phone, it seems that Ray Monroe believed that he had originally been recruited by, and had all along been working for, . . . Phillip Jeffries.

Let me repeat that: Ray Monroe believed he had been recruited by and was working for Phillip Jeffries, a man the Bureau had not seen or heard from since he disappeared from your Philadelphia office in 1989.

I'll take this a step further: I believe it's not only possible, but likely, that the Double went to all that trouble to spring Ray Monroe because he had reason to believe that Monroe would tell him where he could *find* Phillip Jeffries. I also think it's highly probable that after the Double killed Monroe in Montana, he went looking for Jeffries.

Let's pause here long enough to ask ourselves: Why did the Double want to find Jeffries? What did he hope to learn from him? This is where my own scientifically trained mind starts to encounter some pretty hefty cognitive dissonance, but here goes:

By any measure, Jeffries's behavior in your office, in 1989, was damned peculiar. He was shocked to learn what year it was. He said what he said about "Joudy." He also supposedly pointed an accusatory finger at Cooper and, panicked and afraid, shouted something like: "Who do you think this is there?!" He then disappeared—although once again the appropriate esoteric term for something like this is "dis-apparate," *apparate* being the Latin root for "apparition"—not just right in front of your eyes, but also on security tape. Shortly after 10:15 A.M. Almost exactly when Jeffries reappeared—according to eyewitnesses—back in his Buenos Aires hotel, before, not long afterwards, vanishing altogether.

Since this doesn't make sense inside the lines of any rational logic I can support, let me suggest something batshit crazy: What if Jeffries, not unlike Major Briggs a few years later, had gained access to the same system of "portals," holes in dimensional space that allowed him to disappear and reappear, in places far apart in geographical terms, more or less at will? I'll take it one step further, Chief: What if these same portals also allowed him to come *untethered from time*? Wouldn't that help explain why Briggs hadn't aged a day in twenty-five years? Could it also explain how Ray Monroe believed that he was receiving instructions from Phillip Jeffries?

(And as long as we're skating on the thin side of the ice here, what if this not only made it possible to go forward in time, but also backwards? Could that explain the shock and dismay Jeffries exhibited in your office when he learned what year it was?)

After Monroe died, our investigators found a matchbook in his pocket, for a roadside motel called The Dutchman's Lodge, in rural western Montana. I personally visited the address on the matchbook and there's nothing there: It's an empty space on the side of an old two-lane state highway. I then went back and checked historical records for the area and learned that there *was* such a motel at that exact location dating back to the early 1930s. It was built, owned, and operated by a man named Horace "the Dutchman" Vandersant, and it was known not only as a "gateway to a sportsman's paradise," but as a mob- and gangster-friendly establishment—rumor has it John Dillinger once spent a week there while on the lam. The lodge was shut down not long after Vandersant died, in 1962, and was demolished in 1967. For what it's worth—and it could, of course, have been a skillful contemporary reproduction—the matchbook in Monroe's pocket appeared to be relatively new.

There's currently a two-day gap in our knowledge of the Double's movements between when he killed Monroe and when he showed up in Twin Peaks: Is it possible that, after killing Monroe, the Double went to this "Dutchman's Lodge," looking for Phillip Jeffries? (For what it's worth, the lodge's former location lay directly between Missoula and Twin Peaks.) What might the Double have learned there? Was it Jeffries who told him something about the coordinates he'd been given that then sent him on to Twin Peaks? Let me explain why I think this is possible.

If Jeffries is still out in the ether somewhere, in the same way that Briggs was, lost or hiding in some kind of neither-here-nor-there netherworld, could this experience be so assaultive and disorienting to the senses that one consequence is you're never completely sure exactly where or *when* you are? If we view Jeffries's behavior in your office in 1989 through this lens, his alarm at learning *when* he's there becomes, perhaps, more understandable.

For argument's sake, let's assume that, after he killed Monroe and learned about The Dutchman's, the Double and Jeffries had some sort of contact—outside of linear time—at this no-longer-existing rustic Montana lodge. Now let's refocus on Jeffries's alarm at seeing Cooper in 1989—"Who do you think this is there?!"—through this same bizarre lens and this question comes up for me: Did Jeffries think he was seeing not Special Agent Dale Cooper, but the Double?

(At this point, I feel the need to uncategorically state the following: Don't hold me to any of this, Chief. I'm just putting it out there.)

INITIAL TP DATE 9 | 6 | 17

# FEDERAL BUREAU OF INVESTIGATION

CASE #    008-072-0119          BUREAU FILE #    TP-18/18

## TODAY

PRESTON, Tamara

CASE AGENT                    $TP$

INITIAL

# CONFIDENTIAL

FIELD OFFICE CRIMINAL INVESTIGATIVE
AND ADMINISTRATIVE FILES

See also Nos.  011-81-1987      8812

001 43-25

FEDERAL BUREAU
OF INVESTIGATION

*Field Office Criminal Investigative
and Administrative Files*

Here's where it all moves beyond weird, Chief. No sooner has the smoke cleared after that shootout in Sheriff Truman's office, with the Double fading away, and something black and spectral floating out of its body and up through the ceiling—don't even get me going right now on that oddball Cockney kid with the green glove—than the lights go out and you and Cooper, apparently, "apparate" to the basement of the Great Northern Hotel. After a brief exchange, Cooper vanishes in the dark down a long corridor that isn't actually there, the lights come back on, and you're left standing with the Horne brothers in a boiler room.

And, for the *second* time in the past twenty-five years, Special Agent Dale Cooper disappears from sight, sound, and the world as we think we know it.

By the time you get back to the sheriff's station, Diane Evans, Cooper's longtime former assistant (whose mind-altering disappearance-and-doppelganger journey calls for, wouldn't you agree, an exhaustive investigation of its own at some point), who was seen by more than twenty witnesses emerging from a holding cell in the basement only minutes before everything hit the fan in Truman's office, has also now, *without* anyone in that crowded room noticing—including yours truly—once again disappeared without a trace.

So when you jetted off back to Philadelphia later that day and left me to cover the aftermath of what went down in Twin Peaks—my first visit; charming place, as you've always told me, but to be honest, Chief, I'm a big-city girl and always will be—and to mop up, to quote Albert, this "gargantuan multidimensional clusterfuck," I decided to nose around a bit.

This happened today, Chief, just a few hours ago. Up to the minute.

Earlier this morning, while perusing past editions of the *Twin Peaks Post*—outstanding small-town paper, conveniently preserved on microfiche—for more than the fun of it, I went back to look up the occasion of the *first* Cooper disappearance from Twin Peaks. Sure enough, the intrepid *Post* reporting staff, expertly trained by their late editor Douglas Milford, featured his sudden and unexplained departure on their front page, along with pained and puzzled quotes from Cooper's pal Sheriff Harry Truman, about how strange and confusing the whole business was.

You know what else I discovered, Chief, in that same article, a few sentences later? This:

"Agent Cooper had come to town a few months earlier, to aid in the investigation into the disappearance, still unsolved, of local teenage beauty queen, Laura Palmer."

Let me repeat that phrase for you: "still unsolved." No mention of "murder," "wrapped in plastic," or "father arrested for shocking crime eventually dies in police custody of self-inflicted wounds."

It's right there on the front page: **Laura Palmer did not die**. So, fairly certain I've not misplaced my own mind, I go back and check the corresponding police records. They tell me this: Laura Palmer disappeared from Twin Peaks without a trace—on the very same night when, in the world we thought we knew, it *used to be said* she'd died—but the police never found the girl or, if she had been killed elsewhere, her body or made a single arrest. In every subsequent mention in an edition of the *Post,* the case is still listed as an open and pending investigation.

And when I spoke to our good friends at the sheriff's office about this, they all got a slightly dazed and confused expression on their faces when I brought it up, as if they were lost in a fog, having trouble recalling, unable to fully wrap their minds around something that happened so very long ago.

Until finally they said, each and every one of them, "Yeah, that sounds right. That's how I remember it."

I started to examine the public records on the rest of the Palmer family. Their daughter's disappearance dominated the local news for weeks. The same set of suspects was identified and questioned—Jacques Renault, Leo Johnson, Bobby Briggs, James Hurley—as those who were known to have been among the last to see her. No useful information came from them, and no arrests were initially made. The next day, Ronette Pulaski—the girl who was abducted and nearly killed along with Laura, and who had apparently *still* been taken captive—escaped and ended up in the hospital after being found wandering along a railroad trestle, just like "before." But she also testified that Laura had wandered off into the woods before she and Leo and Jacques entered the railroad car.

Laura was never there.

After a while, with a complete lack of tips, leads, or sightings to move an investigation forward, the Laura Palmer story began to fade. Within a month it had gone cold; another "missing person" story with no clear resolution. As mentioned, I did find a few stories in the *Post* about Agent Cooper coming to town to investigate Laura's disappearance—there are not many details to speak of, and he didn't stay long—and nothing much beyond that. (As soon as I return to the office, I intend to look into whether any of Cooper's files or tapes that are still in our possession support this alternate version of events.)

I kept moving forward, searching for more information about the Palmer family. The following year, on February 24, 1990—the one-year anniversary of her "disappearance"—Leland Palmer committed suicide. Alone, with a licensed handgun, in his car, parked near the waterfall by the big hotel. The usual outpouring of shock, grief, and "we never saw this coming" stories appeared in the local press. The act was generally attributed to "a father's overwhelming grief about the unresolved disappearance of his only child." Checking police records, I found that there were at least three visits paid to the Palmer house during that intervening year—all by Sheriff Harry Truman—but no further details about the reasons for them are available, and neither is Sheriff Truman.

I decided to look at the history of the mother; with her being Laura's only living relative now, there was scarcely anywhere else to look.

Sarah Judith Novack Palmer.

I searched all the way back to her childhood in New Mexico, where the family moved—months after her birth in Bellevue, Washington—in the summer of 1943. Her father was a Defense Department employee who had been transferred there to work in some small but unspecified subcontractor role on the Manhattan Project. The family lived outside Los Alamos, in a new suburb built on the edge of the desert specifically for workers involved in the program. Nothing about their family life during that time particularly stands out, unless you count the first successful nuclear bomb test—code name "Trinity"—which took place at White Sands, New Mexico, on July 16, 1945. You know the rest of that story: Less than a month later, atomic bombs were dropped on Hiroshima and Nagasaki and the war with Japan was over.

The Novacks decided to stay on in the area—her father still working for the Defense Department—and as far as the public record is concerned, the rest of Sarah's childhood passed uneventfully. But eleven years later, on August 6, 1956, there was a curious incident that I found reported in the local newspaper. That night, about fifteen miles outside of the town where the Novacks lived, an AM radio station was viciously and mysteriously attacked. Two employees—a receptionist and a nighttime DJ—were found dead inside the building, their heads crushed in particularly gruesome fashion by what forensics called "extreme blunt force trauma."

Included in the accounts that followed over the next few days: half a dozen sightings of strange solitary figures in the area that night, on the road, with at least two placing them in the vicinity of the radio station. Details are sketchy— it was a dark, moonless night—but they sound like drifters or, as one witness called them, "hobos."

Also reported that night: Shortly after the time they believe this attack took place, the station abruptly went off the air. At which point more than a few people reported hearing strange "electrical or mechanical word sounds" com- ing over their radios for about the next six minutes. During this period, many local residents reported severe disturbances among their pets or livestock. A number of others—although only a few are named in the reporting—claimed that members of their family blacked out when they heard these transmissions. When the sounds stopped, just as abruptly as they'd started, and the station went to dead air—which, when they were unable to raise anyone there on the phone, prompted police to head to the station—all of these people immedi- ately regained consciousness, with no memory of the event.

Two of the people named in that account lived in the Novacks' neighbor- hood. Sarah Novack was one of them: According to her parents, they found Sarah unconscious and unresponsive in her upstairs bedroom. She came around in the backseat as they were rushing her to the hospital. According to the newspaper report, emergency room doctors found nothing wrong with the girl—it was the same with all of those they looked at that night; the paper suggests it was close to a dozen people—and she was released after a cur- sory examination.

What to make of it? I have no idea, do you? This may not mean anything, either, but all of this took place a few hours away from the air base at Roswell, where, as we know from the dossier, a young army officer named Doug Milford allegedly witnessed the mysterious "UFO" crash nine years earlier.

Sarah's life rolled on uneventfully. She attended college back in Washington State, where she met the man who would become her husband, and later gave birth to their only child, Laura. After Laura's disappearance, Sarah experienced bouts of severe depression and was treated for it, as previously reported. In the years since—at least in the version where her husband commits suicide—according to medical records she has battled alcoholism, addiction to prescription drugs, and social isolation.

Oh, and in the past year, right around the time Cooper disappeared again and time took a vacation, she was named and questioned as an eyewitness to a particularly gruesome and mysterious death in a disreputable Twin Peaks dive, where a man on the barstool next to her dropped dead with most of his neck missing.

\* \* \*

Chief, I'm glad I've written all this down rapidly, because my own thoughts about every one of these events are growing fuzzier and more indistinct the longer I stay here, creeping into my mind like a mist. I can feel a kind of mental lassitude physically advancing on me. Something's wrong; whether it's with me or this place, I don't know and I don't really care anymore. I need to pull the emergency brake, right now, and get the hell out of here. I've booked a flight back to Philadelphia tomorrow.

INITIAL _T P_   DATE _9 / 6 / 17_

# FINAL THOUGHTS

I'm on the plane now, in the air, forty minutes east of Spokane. The uncanny penumbra I reported hasn't left me—I barely slept—but it's fading as I travel farther east. I don't know what to make of it.

You wanted to know what happened there in that town and region, to these people you knew, whom I feel I've come to know now as well. They meant something to you for a reason, I think, beyond just your knowing them, beyond that they were good or interesting people in their own right: because it was all there, in that one town. All of life, cradle to grave, every shade and color of the spectrum, like a fractal, itself made up of infinite parts. The ocean in a drop of water.

I feel like I laid my hand on a third rail that should be of concern to all of us: that a core fundamental of human existence is wonder—and its analogue is fear. You can't have one without the other, flip sides of the coin.

And even as we "wonder" at what we're doing here, so do we also fear—so deep down below the surface of our lives that few can bear to look at it—that life is a meaningless jest, an extravagant exercise in morbidity, a tale of sorrow and suffering lit by flashes, and made bearable only by moments of companionship and unsustainable joy. Along the way, as we struggle to come to terms and comprehend why this strange fate has befallen us, time becomes no longer our ally—the spendthrift assumption of our youth—but our executioner. It all feels at times like a merciless joke made at our expense, without our consent.

Is the evil in us real? Is it an intrinsic part of us, a force outside us, or nothing more than a reflection of the void? How do we hold both fear and wonder in the mind at once? Does staring into this darkness offer up an answer, or resolution? What does it give us to hold on to? Does it reveal anything at all?

Or can the simple, impossible act of persisting to look at what's in front of us finally pierce the blackness and reward us with a glimpse of something eternal beyond? Is that "heaven"? How do we manage it? The only answer I can console myself with is this: What if the truth lies just beyond the limits of our fear, and the only way to reach it is to never look away? What if that's why we must keep going, why we can never quit trying to overcome it in every moment we're alive?

Look at all that's happened here. One town. The commonplace, familiar, and ordinary—everything we think we know, until you sense the deep, unsettling strangeness informing all of it. How easy it is to quit, give up, lower our eyes. Look at what happens to anyone here who lost the fight, many of whose stories we both now know so well. How recklessly, stupidly we toss away this one chance we have, simply squander it, money down the drain, a thousand different ways. We're holding the coin of the realm in our hands the whole time and we can't even see it.

What I've learned from this place and about these people terrifies me, I'll frankly admit that. How much of what I know, what I've been culturally attuned to believe, feels like the set of a play on a strange stage I've wandered onto without knowing why I'm here. I don't know the lines, I don't know what part I'm playing, I don't even know what the play's about or what it's called. I'm just here onstage, stuck in a dream, lights shining in my eyes. Is anyone out there watching? The play stumbles ahead, feels like artifice, mistakes, frippery, an endless series of false starts, bad assumptions, all the while shadowed with the constant horror that something unforeseen could drop down on me from above or lurch in from the wings at any moment, that the floor could open beneath me and instantly erase even this small, pitiful existence, put out the lights for good.

Chief, this has changed me. You predicted that, and I should have known you'd be right, but you can't know what you don't know until you do. It's because you've already been through it, I think. Does this feeling end? Can you tell me you come out the other side to some kind of understanding, or do I have to take that as another article of faith? There's only one redeeming feeling I can cling to, provided I ever get that far—and I'm not saying I'm there yet, by any stretch—but when it's all stripped away and you realize you're the only one who can put the pieces of yourself together, by yourself, alone—no easy answers from a book, song, or movie or the reassuring words of someone older and "wiser"—I'm noticing it has a tendency to focus and sharpen the mind, and strengthen the will to live constantly with all my senses wide-open to the here and now.

One clear idea emerges from that crucible, forged and hard as rolling steel:

We mustn't give up.

Ever.

INITIAL *T P*  DATE 9 / 6 / 17

feeling I can cling to, provided I ever get that far—and I'm not saying I'm there yet, by any stretch—but when it's all stripped away and you realize you're the only one who can put the pieces of yourself together, by yourself, alone—no easy answers from a book, song, or movie or the reassuring words of someone older and "wiser"—I'm noticing it has a tendency to focus and sharpen the mind, and strengthen the will to live constantly with all my senses wide-open to the here and now.

One clear idea emerges from that crucible, forged and hard as rolling steel:

We mustn't give up.

Ever.

INITIAL TP  DATE 9 | 6 | 17